THE PINBALLS

Other APPLE PAPERBACKS
you will want to read:

THE PINBALLS

by

BETSY BYARS

AN
APPLE
PAPERBACK

SCHOLASTIC BOOK SERVICES
New York Toronto London Auckland Sydney Tokyo

ISBN: 0-590-32427-6

12 11 10 9 8 7 6 5 4 3 2   3 4 5 6/8

Printed in the U.S.A.   11

For David Atchley

1

One summer two boys and a girl went to a foster home to live together.

One of the boys was Harvey. He had two broken legs. He got them when he was run over by his father's new Grand Am.

The day of his accident was supposed to be one of the happiest of Harvey's life. He had written an essay on "Why I Am Proud to Be an American," and he had won third prize. Two dollars. His father had promised to drive him to the meeting and watch him get the award. The winners and their parents were going to have their pictures taken for the newspaper.

When the time came to go, Harvey's father said, "What are you doing in the car?" Harvey had been sitting there, waiting, for fifteen minutes. He was wearing a tie for the first time in his life. "Get out, Harvey, I'm late as it is."

"Get out?"

"Yes, get out."

Harvey did not move. He sat staring straight ahead. He said, "But this is the night I get my award. You promised you'd take me."

"I didn't *promise*. I said I would if I could."

"No, you promised. You said if I'd quit bugging you about it, you'd take me. You promised." He still did not look at his father.

"Get out, Harvey."

"No."

"I'm telling you for the last time, Harvey. Get out."

"Drive me to the meeting and I'll get out."

"You'll get out when I say!" Harvey's father wanted to get to a poker game at the Elks Club, and he was already late. "And I say you get out *now*." With that, the father leaned over, opened the door, and pushed Harvey out of the car.

Harvey landed on his knees in the grass. He jumped to his feet. He grabbed for the car door. His father locked it.

Now Harvey looked at his father. His father's face was as red as if it had been turned inside out.

Quickly Harvey ran around the front of the car to try and open the other door. When he was directly in front of the car, his father accidentally threw the car into drive instead of reverse. In that wrong gear, he stepped on the gas, ran over Harvey and broke both his legs.

The court had taken Harvey away from his father and put him in the foster home "until such time as the father can control his drinking and make a safe home for the boy."

The second boy was Thomas J. He didn't know whom he belonged to. When he was two years old someone had left him in front of a farmhouse like he was an unwanted puppy. The farmhouse belonged to two old ladies, the Benson twins, who were then eighty-two years old. They were the oldest living twins in the state. Every year on their birthday they got letters of congratulation from the governor. They were exactly alike except that one's eyes, nose and mouth were a little bigger than the other's. They looked like matching salt-and-pepper shakers.

Thomas J had stayed with the twins for six years. The twins had meant to take him into town and tell the authorities, but they had kept putting it off. First it was because he was pleasant company, later because he was good help in the garden.

When the twins broke their hips at age eighty-eight, Thomas J was discovered for the first time by the authorities. Nobody knew who he was or where he had come from. He was sent to the foster home "until such time as his real identity can be established or permanent adoptive parents located."

The girl was Carlie. She was as hard to crack as a coconut. She never said anything polite. When anyone asked how she was, she answered "What's it to you?" or "Bug off." Her main fun was watching television, and she threw things at people who blocked her view. Even the dog had been hit with *TV Guide* when he stepped in front of the set when Sonny and Cher were singing "I Got You, Babe."

Carlie had to go to the foster home because she couldn't get along with her stepfather. She had had two stepfathers, but the new one, Russell, was the worst. He was mean to everybody in the family, but especially to Carlie. He resented everything she did.

Once he had hit her so hard when she wouldn't tell him where she'd been that she had gotten a concussion. Even with a concussion she had struggled up and hit him with a double boiler. "Nobody hits me without getting hit back," she had said before she collapsed.

Carlie was to stay at the foster home "until the home situation stabilizes."

"Stabilizes!" Carlie had said to the social worker in charge of her case. "What does that mean?"

"It means until your mother and your stepfather work out their problems."

"Whoo," Carlie said, "that means I'll stay until I'm ready for the old folks home."

The first thing Carlie did when she got to the foster home was pull the plastic footrest up close to the TV. "Don't talk to me when 'Young and Restless' is on," she warned the foster mother, who was standing behind her.

"I just wanted to welcome you," Mrs. Mason said. She put one hand on Carlie's back.

Carlie shook it off. "Welcome me during the commercial," she said.

2

Carlie had been suspicious of people since the day she was born. She swore she could remember being dropped on the floor by the doctor who delivered her.

"You weren't dropped," her mother had told her.

"All right then, why is my face so flat? Was I *ironed*?"

Carlie also claimed that when she was two months old a baby-sitter had stolen a golden cross from around her neck.

"No baby-sitter stole a gold cross from you," her mother had told her.

"All right then, where is it?"

Carlie believed everyone was out to do her in, and she had disliked Mrs. Mason, the foster mother, as soon as she had seen her standing in the doorway.

"I knew she'd have on an apron," Carlie said to the social worker. "She's trying to copy herself after Mrs. Walton — unsuccessfully, I might add."

"Maybe she has on the apron because she was cooking, Carlie."

"*I* should be the social worker. I'm not fooled by things like aprons."

She also didn't like the Masons' living room. "This is right out of 'Leave It to Beaver,'" she said. She especially distrusted the row of photographs over the fireplace. Seventeen pictures of — Carlie guessed — seventeen foster children.

"Well, my picture's not going up there," she grumbled to herself. "And nobody better snap me when I'm not looking either." She sat.

Mrs. Mason waited until "Young and Restless" was over and then she said, "Carlie?"

"I'm still here."

"Well, come on and have some lunch. Then afterward you can help me get the boys' room ready."

Carlie turned. She looked interested for the

first time. "The boys?" she asked. "There're going to be some boys here?"

"Yes, two boys are coming this afternoon — Thomas J and Harvey."

"How old?"

"Eight and thirteen."

"Oh, boo, too young." Carlie got up from the footstool. "What's wrong with them?"

"Wrong with them?"

"Yeah, why do they have to be here? I'm here because I got a bum stepfather. What's their trouble?"

"Well, I guess they'll have to tell you that."

Carlie lifted her hair up off her neck. "How about the thirteen-year-old?" she asked. "What's he like? Big for his age, I hope."

"He has two broken legs. That's about all I can tell you."

"Well," Carlie said, "that lets out dancing."

Carlie was sitting in front of the television when Harvey arrived. He had to be carried in because of his legs. They set the wheelchair down by Carlie's footstool.

She looked around. "What happened to your legs?" she asked. She was interested in medical matters.

He said, "Nothing."

"Well, *something* must have happened. They don't just put casts on your legs for the fun of it. In fact they *won't* put casts on your legs unless you've had a real accident. I know, because a friend of mine tried to get a cast put on her ankle so she wouldn't have to be in Junior Olympics, and they wouldn't do it." She waited, then she said, "So what happened?"

There was a long pause. Harvey looked down at his legs. In his mind the shiny Grand Am lunged over him again. He felt sick. He said, "If you must know, I broke my legs playing football."

He wished it had happened that way. A boy at school had broken his ankle playing football, and everyone in school had autographed his cast. Girls had even kissed the cast and left their lipstick prints.

Harvey's casts were as white as snow. He wished he had thought to forge some names on them. "Love and kisses from Linda." "Best wishes to a wonderful English student from Miss Howell."

Carlie was still looking at him, eyeing the casts, his toes sticking out the end. Then she glanced up at his face.

"What position were you playing?"

Harvey hesitated. "Quarterback," he said.

Carlie snorted. "You're no quarterback. I've seen Joe Namath in person." She looked him over. "If you were playing football at all, you were probably the ball."

Harvey kept looking at his legs.

Carlie decided to give him one more chance. "So what really happened?"

"I was playing football," he insisted.

"Listen," Carlie said. "This is one of my favorite shows, so if you're going to tell me a bunch of big lies about what happened to your legs, well, I'll just go back to watching my show."

"Go back to watching it," Harvey said.

3

Thomas J arrived after supper. He had been living with the Benson twins so long that he yelled everything. That was the only way he could be heard at the Bensons'. The twins were almost deaf.

"Where do I put my things?" he yelled at Mrs. Mason.

"Why, right back here, Thomas J. I'm putting you and Harvey in the same room so you can help him if he needs it."

"I'll be glad to," he yelled. He was used to helping people.

"If Harvey has any trouble in the night, you can call me."

"I'll call you."

"He's sure got the voice for it," Carlie said.

"Do I put my things in the drawer or just leave them in the suitcase?"

Carlie spun around on the footstool. "Will you keep your voice down. I can hardly hear the television."

"I'll be glad to," Thomas J yelled.

That night the three of them sat watching "Tony Orlando and Dawn."

"Now, this really is one of my favorite shows," Carlie said as soon as it was announced. She gave each of them a long hard look.

Thomas J nodded. Actually he would rather have watched something else. The show brought back sad memories. It had been one of the Benson twins' favorites. The twins had always liked anything that came in pairs — doublemint-gum commercials brought them hobbling — and Dawn in their matching dresses looked like twins even though they weren't.

"Sing the song, girls," Tony Orlando said, stepping back on his high-heeled shoes.

Thomas J felt awful. He could remember the twins leaning forward on their canes, trembling a little as they squinted at Dawn. They had the oldest television set in Macon

County, and they had to lean close to see anything.

He hoped there was a TV set at the hospital where they had been taken. They had both broken their hips on the same day. They had been coming in from the garden — Thomas J had been right behind them carrying a bushel of weeds — when one of them had slipped. She had grabbed the other for support, and they both had gone down on the path. One had broken her right hip; the other, her left.

It was not until they were being admitted to the hospital that Thomas J had learned their first names. For six years he had just called them both Aunt Benson. Their first names were Thomas and Jefferson. They had been named for their father's favorite president. That was how he had gotten the name Thomas J. He had been named for them.

"Don't worry, Thomas J," they had told him in the emergency room where they had lain on side-by-side tables, "we'll get over this, won't we, Sister?"

"*I* will."

"We *both* will because everybody in our family has lived to be at least ninety."

Thomas J had nodded. He knew their father had lived to be ninety-six. The father would have lived longer except that a limb fell off a tree and hit him on the head. The twins had kept the limb on the back porch for a long while, and the only time the twins had ever been angry at Thomas J was when he, not knowing the importance of the limb, had broken it up for firewood.

Andy Griffith was on the television now, telling a long joke. Carlie said, "Why doesn't he get off? Nobody wants to listen to him."

"I do," Harvey said.

Carlie glanced at him. "You would," she said.

Harvey felt a twinge in his right leg. It was the worst of the breaks. The bone had gone through the skin.

He looked at the back of Carlie's head. He would have liked to answer her back, to insult her, but he knew that Carlie could out-insult anybody he had ever met.

"He *gives* me a pain," Carlie said. She glanced around the room, taking in everyone present. "And he's not the only one."

4

Carlie entered her room slowly. It was the
first time she had slept in a room by herself.
At one time in her life she had slept with a
cousin, her stepfather's two daughters and a
half sister, all in one bed. She had spent her
nights saying "Move over, will you?" and
"Who do you think you are — Miss America?"

She walked slowly over to the dresser and
looked at herself in the mirror. She had de-
veloped a way of smiling that hid her crooked
lower teeth. She smiled at herself now, making sure she still had the technique.

Suddenly she heard a noise behind her. She
swirled around. She didn't like anybody
watching her when she was looking at herself.

When she saw it was Thomas J, she could have stung him. "What are you staring at?"

"Nothing. I just wanted to tell you I found your earring." He came in with a small pleased smile. He was thin and walked as carefully as an old person. He held out the earring.

When Carlie had discovered one of her earrings was missing just after "Tony Orlando and Dawn," she had accused everyone in the house of stealing it. "I'm going to find that earring if I have to turn every one of you upside down and shake you," she had said. "That earring is pure gold."

"Now, now, Carlie, no one stole your earring," Mrs. Mason had said.

"All right then, where is it?"

"The earring was in the bathroom," Thomas J said, still smiling. "It was by the basin." He held it out. He had been as pleased when he found it as if it had been a gold nugget. He couldn't wait to bring it to her. Once when he had found the Bensons' father's gold watch, they had been so happy they had patted him. It was the only time the Benson twins had ever touched him on purpose. He could still remember their stiff old fingers tapping his head.

"Good boy," they had said. It had made him

feel warm and happy. He had wanted them to lose the watch over and over again so he could keep finding it, the way a dog keeps fetching a stick.

Also he wanted Carlie to like him. He admired her. Her long flowing hair — lion-colored — made him aware of his own scraggly head. The Benson twins always cut his hair together, one on each side, neither bothering to stop and check the other's work. As he came toward her, he smoothed his hair.

Carlie snatched the earring from him and looked at it suspiciously. "So you just *found* it, huh?"

He didn't get her meaning. "Yes, it was by the basin. I looked down and there it was. It was like the time the Benson twins lost their father's watch and I —"

"Huh, strange that you just happened to find it after I announced I was going to search everybody's room."

Now he got her meaning. "Oh, I didn't steal it. Really I didn't. I found it. It was by the basin. Honest." His voice got even louder. "You can ask Mrs. Mason if you don't believe me. She heard me find it."

Carlie put the earring back on her ear. "I tell you one thing. I'm having my ears pierced as soon as possible. That's the only way things are going to be safe around here."

"I found it, I tell you," Thomas J yelled. He took two steps backward. "I found it!"

"All right, all right, you found it," Carlie said. She glanced at the open door. "Keep your voice down." She turned back to the mirror. "I guess even a blind pig can come up with an acorn every now and then."

After Thomas J left, Carlie got into bed and stared up at the ceiling. Mrs. Mason passed by in the hall and stuck her head in the door. "Everything all right, Carlie?"

"What do you think?" Carlie said.

"Oh, I imagine things seem very wrong tonight."

"*Seem?*" Carlie said.

Mrs. Mason came in and stood by the bed. She patted Carlie's arm. "The first night is always the hardest."

Carlie was silent.

Mrs. Mason sat on the edge of the bed. "And I know how you feel."

"How do you know? Have you ever been in a foster home?"

"I've had a lot of kids staying with me — seventeen, not counting you three — and all seventeen told me that the first night was the worst. They all said they just felt sick." She kept her hand on Carlie's arm. "I guess 'home sickness' is a very real kind of illness, like measles or mumps."

"Too bad there's not a vaccine."

"Yes."

"Only the people that give money for vaccines, they want to give for heart diseases and polio, stuff *their* kids might get. Nobody worries about us."

"Yes, they do, Carlie."

"Anyway the only reason I came was because Russell — that's my stepfather — threatened to cut off all my hair. And it took me since fourth grade to grow this hair!" She yanked the sheet up higher on her shoulders. "Now, I wonder if it was worth it."

"Carlie, did you see the pictures of the kids in the living room?"

"How could I miss?"

"Well, all of those kids have gone on into the world. Two of them are in college now. They write me letters. One has his own service station. Some are back with their families. It all works out somehow." She smiled. "Even without a vaccine."

She waited for a moment and patted

Carlie's arm again. Then she rose from the bed. "Things'll be better tomorrow. You'll see."

"They better be," Carlie answered as Mrs. Mason left the room. She turned her face to the wall. She thought, I can always run away.

5

Harvey and Thomas J shared the room across the hall. It had bunk beds. Because of his broken legs Harvey got the bottom bunk. He eased himself down on the mattress and looked up at the springs.

Thomas J paused beside the bed. Every night at the Bensons' he had said his prayers like the twins did — on his knees beside the bed, arms out straight as boards, fingers pointed up. He felt shy about praying in front of Harvey.

"What are you standing there for?" Harvey asked, glancing at him.

"Nothing."

Still Thomas J hesitated. The habit to pray was strong. Harvey was still looking at him, waiting. Abruptly Thomas J climbed up the ladder to his bed.

"Do you want to know how I broke my legs?" Harvey asked.

Thomas J was on his knees in the upper bunk. "Yes," he answered.

"I was playing football — quarterback — and I got tackled too hard." He stared down at his casts, at his pink toes. "Everyone was going to autograph my casts — all my friends — but I had to come here before they could."

"That's too bad," Thomas J said. He was still in praying position, but he eased back onto his heels. "You know, bones break very easily. You can break bones just walking down a path."

"Oh, I don't know about that," Harvey said.

"Yes, it really can happen." Thomas J leaned over the edge of the bunk and looked at Harvey. "The Benson twins — that's who I lived with before I came here — both broke their hips just walking down a path to the house. They slipped."

"Oh, well, yeah, sure, if they slipped."

"That's why I had to come here. They're both in the hospital."

"I had to come here because there was no one at home to take care of me."

"How about your mother?"

"My mom doesn't live with us anymore."

"Oh." Thomas J waited, watching Harvey, but Harvey had no more to say. After a moment Thomas J withdrew to his bunk.

On the bottom bed, Harvey lay without moving. Harvey had not seen his mother in three years. She had gone to Virginia to live in a commune with nineteen other people and find herself by getting back to nature.

Harvey could still remember the last terrible quarrel between his parents.

"I *know* you cannot understand my having to leave," his mother had said. Harvey had crouched on the stairs, peering around the corner from time to time at the twisted angry faces. Their faces looked gnarled enough to put on a cathedral. "But I have to find myself. I — "

"Find yourself! What does that mean? The man who invented the term 'find yourself' ought to be locked up in a mental hospital."

"It means I don't know who I am anymore. I have no identity."

"You're my wife, isn't that identity enough? You're Harvey's mother! And remember, you were the one who wanted a kid so much. I said 'Let's wait,' but, oh, no, you — "

"I want to be *me*."

"Well, be you! Be anything you want to be! Just don't go running off to some fool place in Virginia where people run around naked."

"They don't run around naked. They're very caring people. They — oh, it's just no use trying to make you understand." His mother was talking through clenched teeth now. "We cannot communicate. We never could."

"I knew this would happen when you started those yoga lessons."

"The yoga classes had nothing to do with this. I'm just trying to — "

"And that Maharishna, or whatever he called himself — I suppose he had nothing to do with it either!"

"It's no use talking to you. You could never understand in a million years."

Harvey had crept back up the stairs then. He couldn't understand either. He just hoped that his mother would return in a week or two, having found herself. He imagined her floating in like Mother Nature with daisies in her hair and peace in her heart.

She had never come back. The only thing he had seen of her was a picture in the *New York Times Magazine*. She and some of the other people had been pictured on their Virginia farm. His mother had been weaving a hammock with two men. They had looked so much alike, the two men and his mom, that Harvey had had a hard time picking her out.

His father had thrown the whole *New York Times* in the fireplace when he saw it and had drunk martinis until he passed out on the sofa.

On the upper bunk Thomas J finished his prayer. He lay down on the stiff, clean sheet. "Well, good-night," he called down.

"Good-night," Harvey answered.

6

It was morning, and Harvey's legs hurt. He didn't feel like getting out of bed, and so Mrs. Mason sent Carlie in with a breakfast tray.

"I wish someone would bring *me* a tray," Carlie said as she entered. She set it on his bedside table. She stood staring down at him.

Harvey looked at the tray.

"It's Little Crunchies," Carlie said. "They'll make you big and strong." She looked at him. "Although in your case it's going to take more than Little Crunchies, if you ask me. I wonder if they make Big Crunchies."

Harvey said nothing.

She put one hand on her hip. "Whoo," she said, "if someone brought me a breakfast tray I wouldn't just lie there like a rope."

Harvey said nothing.

"If somebody brought me a breakfast tray I'd drop over dead."

She waited.

Then she said, "You don't get anything, do you, Harvey? I just gave you the perfect chance to insult me. I just said, 'If somebody brought me a breakfast tray, I'd drop over dead.' Now you should say, 'Is that a promise?'"

Carlie waited. Then she said, "I give up. You're hopeless."

She started from the room. "When you get through eating — if you ever do — call and the slave of the world will come back for your tray."

Carlie was all the way out the door when he said, "Thank you, Carlie."

Carlie stopped. She stood motionless in the hall for a moment. Then she said, "No need to thank *slaves*."

She kept standing there. She felt Harvey had only thanked her to make her feel bad. And he had succeeded. For some reason, insults didn't hurt her. People could insult her all day long, and she would insult them right back. But let somebody say something polite or nice to her — it made her feel terrible.

Carlie looked across at the opposite wall.

The phone was there, and she walked over slowly. Suddenly she wanted to make a long-distance call. Not to her mother, she decided. She wanted to call somebody like Cher or Rhoda or Mary Tyler Moore.

"Hi," she would say, "this is Carlie. Let me tell you the rotten thing that happened to me."

She was staring at the phone, wondering how you called a star, when Mrs. Mason appeared in the doorway. "Did you take Harvey his tray?"

"Yeah, but he didn't eat."

Mrs. Mason wiped her hands on her apron. "We're going to have to be especially nice to Harvey these next few weeks."

"To *Harvey*?"

"Yes, he's having a rough time of it."

"Well, how about me?" Carlie said. "Why doesn't anybody ever think of being especially nice to me? What do I have to do to get some attention around here — break both *my* legs?"

"Now, Carlie — "

"Would a wrist be enough?"

Mrs. Mason put her hand on Carlie's shoulder. "I just have the feeling you can help Harvey."

"Whoo, are you off base."

"You're a very strong girl, Carlie, whether you know it or not."

"If Harvey's depending on me for help, he is going to go down the drain."

"Listen, Carlie —"

"No, *you* listen. Harvey and me and Thomas J are just like pinballs. Somebody put in a dime and punched a button and out we came, ready or not, and settled in the same groove. That's all." She looked at Mrs. Mason. "Now, you don't see pinballs helping each other, do you?"

"Carlie —"

"They can't. They're just things. They hit this bumper, they go over here. They hit that light, they go over there."

"Carlie —"

"And soon as they get settled, somebody comes along and puts in another dime and off they go again." Carlie was standing by the phone. She reached up and dialed zero. "I can't help Harvey and I can't help myself."

"I think you can," Mrs. Mason said.

"Take a good look at a pinball machine sometime," Carlie said. "You might learn something about life."

In his room Harvey lay without moving. He had heard every word of the conversation. He wished his father had heard it too.

"You kids today got it easy," his father was

always saying. "It was tough when I was a kid — none of this five dollars here and ten dollars there."

Harvey, who asked for money only when he needed it for food, always waited in silence.

His father would rave some more about how easy Harvey had it, and then he would pull some bills from his pocket. He would toss them at Harvey so Harvey would have to pick them up from the floor. Then Harvey's father always ended with "Later you'll find out things aren't so easy, and you'll find out the hard way, like me."

Harvey looked down at his legs. When his father said "the hard way," Harvey thought, he meant the hard way.

Slowly, as if his arms were broken instead of his legs, he began to eat his cereal.

7

After supper the three of them settled in the living room. Thomas J was writing a letter to the Benson twins. It was addressed to Miss Thomas and Miss Jefferson Benson, Sundale Hospital.

It started out:

> Hi,
> How are your hips?

As soon as Harvey had seen Thomas J writing a letter, he had asked for paper too. He was having a hard time getting started on his letter. He didn't want to write to his father, and he didn't know his mother's address in Virginia, but he felt left out not to be writing.

Although he had not put down a word, he kept lifting his head and asking things like "How do you spell 'wonderful'?"

"I hope you're not describing yourself," Carlie said without looking up. She was also writing. The letter was to her mother.

"I'm not saying what I'm describing," Harvey said in a superior manner. His eyebrows were raised.

"Could it be me?" Carlie asked. "Are you by any chance making a list of all the things I am? Wonderful. Exciting. Temptatious. Don't forget to mention that my hair is good enough for a creme-rinse commercial and my skin is so soft no Brillo soap pad can smooth it."

Harvey tried to think of an answer. He couldn't.

Carlie broke off. She looked down at her letter. She bent over it.

Carlie didn't bother with punctuation when she wrote. Her letter went:

Please send for me I won't cause you any trouble I have learned my lesson and anyway it wasn't me who caused the trouble It was Russell From now on I will just keep out of his way I will keep out of everybodys

*way   All I want is to come home   Anyway
Russell hit me harder than I hit him   Talk
to the social worker and tell her everything is
all right   Make everything all right   I want
to come home*

Harvey watched Carlie writing her letter.
He was jealous that she had so much to say.
He still hadn't written a word. He shifted in
his wheelchair. His casts itched and his right
leg hurt.

He thought of writing that to his father,
but he didn't think his father would care
whether his legs itched or hurt or whatever.
In the hospital his father had seemed very
sorry. He actually cried. Real tears. He had
said, "I didn't know. I thought I was in reverse. I just bought the car, see, and I didn't
know."

The tears were not for him, Harvey had
sensed. They were for the doctor and the
pretty nurse and especially for the police who
were charging him with drunken driving.
Harvey had lain there and not shed a tear.

Now suddenly he wished he could cry.
Quickly he crumpled his blank paper. "I don't
feel like writing letters."

Thomas J hovered over his paper. He had

lived with the Benson twins for as long as he could remember, but he couldn't think of anything to write to them. All he still had was "How are your hips?" He lifted his head. "Can you send off a letter with just one sentence in it?" he asked.

"No," Carlie said, "you got to have two. We learned that in English."

"Oh."

"You can always end by saying "There's a wonderful girl here named Carlie who is just like a sister to me." She turned to look at him. "Who's this letter going to, anyway?"

"The Benson twins."

"Boys?"

"No."

"Oh, wrong sex," Carlie said, turning back to her letter.

"They're eighty-eight."

"Wrong age too."

"Next year, if they live, they may get to be in the *Book of World Records*."

"Me too," Carle said. "If I live I'll be the most shifted around juvenile in the world." Carlie finished her letter, ending it with twelve "pleases," all underlined. She put it in an envelope and sealed it. "Well, that's that." She looked around to see whom she could pester.

Harvey was writing at last. He had given up on a letter, but Carlie had given him an idea when she mentioned a list about herself. Now he was making a list about himself. The list was entitled "Bad Things that Have Happened to Me."

Number one was "Appendectomy."

"What are you writing?" Carlie asked, sensing it was something secret. She darted over to take a look. She knew that because of his broken legs, he couldn't get out of the way.

Harvey put the list against his chest. "It's none of your business."

"Everything I'm interested in is my business." She snatched the list from his hand. She read it aloud. "Appendectomy." She looked up. "Hey, have you really had an appendectomy?"

"Yes."

Carlie's eyes narrowed with suspicion. "How big's your scar?"

"About that long."

"I knew it!" she cried. "You know what somebody told me one time? He told me that doctors make real tiny slits and then pull all your guts outside and hold them up to the light so they can work better." She paused. She was delighted. "Which is probably true! And you know how Dr. Welby and all those

TV doctors make incisions! The incisions are that long — fourteen, fifteen inches maybe. They ought to talk to this friend of mine."

She handed the list back to Harvey. It fluttered to his lap like an old leaf.

Carlie said, "I'm going to make some lists about myself. Mine's going to be called 'Big Events and How I Got Cheated out of Them.' "

Carlie leaned back on the sofa and began to count off the bad times on her fingers. "Number one — and this really was a cheat — I was going to be a majorette in Junior High. I even went to Majorette Clinic. Cost my mom fifteen dollars, and then I come to find out that you couldn't even try out if you didn't have good grades. And what does good grades have to do with twirling a baton — tell me that?" She looked from Harvey to Thomas J, whose mouth was hanging open. "What do two E's in English and World Studies and one D-minus in Math have to do with twirling a baton?"

"I don't know," Thomas J said. It was the first time he had spoken softly since he had arrived.

"And then you know what happened? I was all set to try out for Miss Teenaged Lancaster. My talent was baton twirling, which I had already spent fifteen dollars learning in Majorette Clinic.

"Anyway, to make a rotten story short, the week before tryouts, I got attacked by my stepfather and sent over here. I never even had a chance." She put her feet up on the plastic footrest. "What else is on *your* list?" she asked Harvey.

He and Thomas J both looked startled.

"What else is on your 'Bad Things' list?" she urged.

"Nothing. I've just got the appendectomy so far."

"Well, write down two broken legs," Carlie suggested. "I wouldn't exactly call them the fun event of the year." She paused. "If it was me, I'd make that number two *and* three, wouldn't you, Thomas J? Number two, right leg. Number three, left."

"I'm *going* to write them down," Harvey said patiently. "I'm just trying to keep the events in the order they happened."

8

In the backyard of the Mason house were swing sets and play equipment, because several years ago the Masons had had little children living with them. Carlie was on one of the swings, pumping herself so hard the whole swing set was shaking.

Harvey was sitting on the back porch in his wheelchair. He had gotten interested in making as many lists about himself as he could, and Mrs. Mason had bought him a spiral notebook.

He had felt so good about the lists that he had begun to think that if his mother had made some lists about herself — well, maybe she could have found her identity without going off to make hammocks in Virginia.

Carlie stopped swinging. She walked over to the sandbox. "Want to see me make a froggie house?" she asked Harvey.

"No."

"Why, Harvey, I thought all little kiddies liked to watch people make froggie houses."

"Well, maybe little kiddies do."

"Harvey, does this mean you're no longer a little kiddie? Have you passed into puberty while I wasn't looking?" She piled damp sand over her foot, eased her foot out and shook off the sand. "There. Now during the night, Harvey, a little froggie will come and live in this house." She got up. "Oh, I'm bored," she said. She stepped on the sand house and came over to the porch. She sat down on the steps. "Harvey?"

"What?"

"Have you ever thought of running away?"

He looked down at his broken legs. "Hardly," he said.

She grinned. "Harvey?"

"Now what?"

"Have you ever thought of *rolling* away?" He didn't answer.

"I think about it all the time," she said, looking down at her feet.

There was a silence, then Harvey cleared

his throat and said, " 'Young and Restless' is on television." He found it hard to concentrate on his lists when Carlie was around. At any moment she might snatch the book from his hand. He especially did not want her to see that she was number three on the list of people he was afraid of.

"I *know* 'Young and Restless' is on," she said. "I'm getting sick of that show."

Actually the reason Carlie wasn't watching television was because the mail had just come and there had been no letter from her mother. Eight days and not even a postcard.

"What's this list about?" Carlie asked.

"It's called 'Books That I Have Enjoyed.' "

"Oh." Carlie was disappointed.

"I've already got eighteen and I'm just getting started."

"I could make up my list in two seconds. *Hong Kong Nurse.* That's the only really good book I ever read. You ought to try it. After that I read *Peace Corps Nurse* and *Nurse of the Yukon,* but they weren't as good. Not enough romance."

"Carlie, would you help me with lunch?" Mrs. Mason called from the kitchen.

"The slave of the world is being summoned," Carlie said. She got up slowly. She saw that Harvey had written two more titles on his list.

Harvey did not glance up. He was really enjoying this list. It didn't bring back any unpleasant memories, not like the list called "Promises My Mother Broke." That list had almost made him cry. Almost but not quite. It wasn't as easy to cry as people thought.

Carlie walked to the door. "There was one other book I wanted to read — *Appalachian Nurse* — but I never could find it in the library. The good books are always checked out."

Harvey was still writing.

At the door Carlie paused. "Harvey, when I do run away, will you miss me?"

"I don't know."

"I'll give you a sample of life without me." She went into the kitchen, then she called out the window, "Pretty bad, isn't it, Harvey?"

He didn't look up.

9

Mr. Mason was driving Thomas J into Maidsville to visit the Benson twins in the hospital.

"Can I come too?" Carlie asked.

"Not this time."

"But I got a cousin in Maidsville," she lied. "She runs a boutique and I want to see what kind of stuff she's got."

"You can go another time," Mrs. Mason said. "They're just going straight to the hospital and back."

"Then I'll just go straight to the boutique and back," Carlie went on.

Harvey said, "Could I go? That's just about seven blocks from my house."

"No, Harvey," Mrs. Mason said in a gentler voice.

"But I wouldn't go home. I just want to

stop at the Kentucky Fried Chicken place right across from the hospital. I could get some chicken while they're visiting."

"No."

"I wouldn't be any trouble." Harvey moved forward in his wheelchair.

Harvey was addicted to Kentucky Fried Chicken. He ate it every night that his father didn't get home for supper. Once he had eaten it thirty-two nights in a row.

He would pedal over on his bike, put the red-and-white-striped box in his bicycle basket and pedal home. He would eat in front of the TV watching his favorite programs. Now the thought of eating in his own living room made his mouth water for the chicken and the little cups of mashed potatoes and gravy.

"No."

"Well, if you get a chance," he rolled closer to Mr. Mason, "would you please bring me a box of chicken? *Please!* This is important."

"That's a good idea," Mrs. Mason said. "Get a bucket of chicken. It's too hot to cook."

"If we have time," Mr. Mason said.

Carlie and Harvey and Mrs. Mason stayed at the door watching Thomas J and Mr. Mason get in the car. Then Mrs. Mason turned.

"Well, how about it, Carlie?" she said. "You ready to learn to sew today?"

Carlie groaned. "I tried it once. I made an apron in Home Ec and I got a C-minus on it because the gathers were bunched. You have to have a certain kind of hands to sew."

"Nonsense. I had two girls with me last year, and I taught them to sew in one afternoon. They made all kinds of nice clothes. Their pictures are on the mantel in the dresses they made."

"What happened to them?"

"The sisters?"

"Yes."

"Why, they went home — left two days before you and the boys got here. I hardly had time to change the sheets."

"So that really happens sometimes — that people get to go home?"

"Yes, it really happens." Mrs. Mason smiled. "Now, come on. We'll start on a real easy halter top."

"Come on, Harvey," Carlie said. Harvey was still at the door looking down the empty street. "Don't you want to see me in misery?" She followed Mrs. Mason down the hall. "You know, I wish *I* had a twin," she said. "Then we could go around fooling people; like if some boy liked my twin, then I could pretend to be her and say all kinds of crazy things. It would really be fun to have a twin. She could take tests for me and —" She looked back over her shoulder. "Come *on,* Harvey." She liked an audience. She always did better when people were watching her. "This may be your one and only chance to see me sew and I'm not kidding. Come on."

"All right, what did I do wrong now?" Carlie asked, holding out the halter.

"Let's see." Mrs. Mason put down her own sewing. "Well, you took a dart on this side and you didn't take one over here. That's why it doesn't fit." Mrs. Mason began to take out Carlie's seam.

Carlie watched Mrs. Mason rather than what she was doing. After a moment she said, "Do you mind if I ask you something?"

"No, go ahead."

"Well, why didn't you have children of your own, that's what I'm wondering, instead of taking in strays?"

"I don't think of you as strays, Carlie." Mrs. Mason smiled. She put a pin into the cloth and then lowered it to her lap. "I did want children of my own—lots of them. My sister Helen has four children, Liz has five, but as it turned out, I couldn't have any." She picked up the cloth. "Now, Carlie, see, I've pinned the dart for you. Sew along this line."

"But why didn't you adopt a child?"

"Well, that's what we were going to do. We even had our papers in. Only while we were waiting — this was a long time ago — they asked us to be foster parents. I didn't want to at first, but — "

"Why not? I'm curious."

"Well, I knew I would come to love the child and I knew the child would leave, and I didn't think I could stand it. I wanted, you know, a child of my OWN, capital letters, who would never leave. Only nobody has that, Carlie." She straightened. "Anyway, it's worked out, Carlie, not the way I thought when I was your age, not the way I planned, but it has worked out." She smiled. "Now sew your halter."

10

Thomas J sat beside Mr. Mason on the front seat of the car, sliding a little on the plastic covers every time the car went around a curve. He had never visited anyone in a hospital before, and he had a dread about it.

"Why don't you take them some candy?" Carlie had suggested. "That's what I'd want if I was in the hospital."

"They don't believe in candy," Thomas J had answered.

Carlie had stared at him like he didn't have good sense. "Don't believe in candy! How can they not believe in candy? There's Mounds, Mr. Goodbars, Hershey's, Sweetarts, Jujubes. I mean, I can understand how they wouldn't believe in ghosts or something, but candy! How can anybody not believe in candy?"

"They just don't. They don't believe in soda pop. They don't believe in chewing gum."

"Whoo, they are *nuts*." She had paused, then grinned. "Or don't they believe in them either?"

As Thomas J sat there beside Mr. Mason he wished he did have a box of candy on his lap. One of those big silver-wrapped boxes of candy he'd seen in drugstores with a bow and a plastic rose on top. It would make it all easier.

"Here's something for you," he would say. And they, who had never believed in candy, would be overcome. It would be like people who didn't believe in heaven suddenly finding themselves floating upward.

They got to the hospital and walked slowly down the green halls. It was an ugly green to Thomas J, nothing like the greens of nature. Suddenly Thomas J remembered the garden. He remembered the twins working, feeling the tomatoes, pulling off dead leaves, lifting their heads to the sun.

He stumbled in the hall. "It'll be all right," Mr. Mason said. He put his hand on Thomas J's shoulder, not to push him forward, just to help him along, like planes refueling in the air.

"Three-twenty. This must be the room," Mr. Mason said. They entered together.

The Benson twins lay in side-by-side beds, and beyond them was another woman reading a magazine. Thomas J moved between the twins' beds.

The twins didn't look like themselves. They had gotten thinner. They hardly made wrinkles in the covers.

"Hi," Thomas J said.

"Thomas J, is that you?"

"Yes'm." He had been afraid they wouldn't know him. Sometimes at home they had forgotten him. He would go in for supper, and there would only be two places set at the kitchen table. "Why, Thomas J," one of them would cry, "we forgot all about you. Get yourself a plate."

"I'm here for a visit," he added.

"Sister, it's Thomas J."

"I see him."

There was a silence. Then both twins reached out their hands to him. He could never remember holding their hands before, and it made him feel strange. He glanced over his shoulder at Mr. Mason.

"Have you been back to the house?" one of the twins asked.

"Not since I left."

"What?"

He turned back to the twins. *"Not since I left."*

"Don't let things go down."

"Nome."

"The peas are just coming in."

"Yes'm."

"You got to can the peas, Thomas J. You've seen us do it enough to know how."

"I don't remember, though. I don't even know where the jars are at."

"We'll stop by on the way home and check on the peas," Mr. Mason said.

"Get Papa's gold watch," one of the twins — Jefferson — said. "You know where it is."

"Yes'm."

"If people know it's there, they'll break in and steal it. Might have already."

"Yes'm."

"And the gold coins — there's three of them — you know where they're at."

"Under the mattress."

"Under *my* mattress," Jefferson said.

There was a silence. Jefferson closed her eyes. Thomas J cleared his throat. "How are your hips?" he asked.

"They operated on us. Put pins in."

"Oh."

Now both of them closed their eyes. Thomas J took one step forward. He still held their hands.

Suddenly he wanted to ask about that morning, long ago, when he had come tottering up the road. He felt as if this might be his last chance. He had asked them for details before, but all they had said was "You just come up the drive, that's all to tell."

"But what did I have on?"

"Oh, let's see. What was it, Sister?"

"A diaper and a shirt."

"Do you still have them — the diaper and the shirt?" At the time he had thought there might be a clue there — a laundry mark or a name.

"No, we used them for dusting, but I do remember there was a dog's picture on the shirt."

"A dog?"

"Because I've seen him on TV. What is his name, Sister? You know who I'm talking about."

"Lassie?"

"No, a cartoon dog. I'll think of it in a minute. He's white with — "

"But did you go out to the road and look for cars?" he had asked, interrupting.

"Sister did."

"Did she see anybody?"

"No."

"An accident or something?"

"There wasn't a soul in sight."

Later, one night when he was watching a Halloween special on TV, one of the twins had cried, "*That's* the dog. That's the dog that was on your shirt when we found you." It was Snoopy.

The twins were asleep now. Their hands slipped from Thomas J's. Thomas J took a step backward and bumped into Mr. Mason.

"Well, we might as well go, Thomas J," he said.

"All right."

At the foot of Jefferson's bed, even though he knew they couldn't hear him, he said, "I hope your hips get better."

11

It gave Thomas J a sad feeling to go in the Bensons' house. It seemed emptier than a house without any furniture.

He got the watch and the three coins, wrapped them in a handkerchief and put them in his pocket. Then, without looking at Mr. Mason he said, "I want to see how the peas are."

He went to the back door, but he didn't even have to step outside to see the garden was ruined. There had been no rain in three weeks, and the leaves on the plants were yellow. The vines were shriveled and dead. There were no tomatoes.

He and Mr. Mason looked over the sad scene. Mr. Mason said, "When you write the

Bensons, I wouldn't mention the garden. It isn't likely they're going to see it this year anyway."

"I won't." He paused. "I couldn't."

When they were in the car and almost to the main road, Thomas J turned and looked back. "Wait just a minute," he said. Mr. Mason stopped the car.

"Anything wrong?"

"No."

Thomas J felt like this was the last time he would ever see this house. He wanted to imagine himself walking up the drive in a shirt and diaper. Lost. Abandoned. Dirty. Tear streaked probably — being left behind had to make a baby cry.

He tried to imagine the twins waiting on the Porch, arms outstretched, then hurrying down the steps to hug him in his dirty shirt and diaper.

He couldn't get a picture of it. "Let's go," he said.

They were halfway home when they remembered about the Kentucky Fried Chicken.

Harvey was on the front porch waiting for them. When he saw them get out of the car without the red-striped boxes, he felt like crying. He rolled himself back to his room and sat staring out the side window. There was nothing to see there but an uncut field.

"What's wrong with *you*?" Carlie asked from the door. "Is the sight of me in my new halter too much for you?"

"Leave me alone."

"What if I don't want to?"

"Leave me alone!"

Carlie took two steps into the room. "I can't," she said. "I get curious about what's bugging people." She sat down on the bottom bunk. "That's because I'm going to be a nurse when I grow up and treat mentals."

"I'm not a mental."

"Huh, that's what they all say."

"Will you get out of here?"

Carlie stretched out on the bed, her chin resting on her hands. "Tell me what's wrong and I'll decide whether you're a mental or not. Pretend I'm a nurse with a long beard. Tell me all."

Through clenched teeth Harvey said, "If you must know, what's wrong is that I wanted some Kentucky Fried Chicken and I'm not going to get any."

"They didn't get the chicken?" Carlie cried, sitting up. She was disappointed too. She liked bought food much better than home cooked. "I was really looking forward to that chicken."

"Not like me."

"Now we'll probably have hamburgers," Carlie said, "and they won't be Big Macs either, you can bet on that. They'll be *cooked*."

"Carlie," Mrs. Mason called, "give me a hand, will you? We're going to grill some hamburgers in the backyard. It'll be like a picnic."

"See, what'd I tell you?" Carlie said. "I'll probably get grease all over my new halter and I really worked on this thing too. You saw me." At the door she turned and said, "I've judged your case, Harvey." She grinned. "You aren't a mental."

"Thank you," Harvey said.

After the picnic Carlie wanted to cheer Harvey and Thomas J up so she said, "I wish I had somebody to take my picture."

Nobody answered. Thomas J sat without looking up. In his pocket was the Bensons' father's watch and the three gold coins. He had never felt a heavier burden. Harvey didn't look up either. His hamburger had tasted like sawdust. He wanted chicken more than ever.

"They're having a Sonny and Cher look-alike contest," Carlie went on, "and I want to enter."

"You don't look like Cher," Harvey said.

"I know. I'm gonna be Sonny!"

She waited. There was no reaction. "Oh, you guys," she said in a disgusted voice, "what do I have to do to cheer you up?"

"Go in the house," Harvey said.

She spun around and looked at him. She grinned. "You know, Harvey, maybe there's hope for you after all."

12

"What's the list for today?" Carlie asked, sitting down on the back steps.

"Oh, it's a list about disappointments."

"Not another one. That's what all your lists are about."

"I have never done this list before. It's called 'Gifts I Got That I Didn't Want,'" Harvey said. "You know, like I was expecting one thing and got something else."

"That's the story of my life," Carlie said. "I expected a floating opal three years in a row and you don't see it hanging around my neck, do you?" There was a pause and then Carlie said, "What bad gifts did you get?"

"Well, they weren't exactly *bad* — some people would have been pleased with them —

but when my mom lived with us, she'd promised me a puppy for my tenth birthday." He paused. "I really wanted that puppy." He paused again. "My mom and me would look through the newspaper at night and read ads together, you know, like 'Cocker spaniels, wormed and ready to go.' It was the happiest time of my life. I wanted every dog I read about. I couldn't wait for the paper to come at night. I'd sit out on the front steps and wait for it."

"So?" Carlie said.

Harvey looked down at his legs. "So my mom left home right before my birthday. She left on the sixth and my birthday was the seventeenth."

"I thought only fathers left home," Carlie said. "I lost two that way — wish it was three."

"And after that," Harvey went on, "my dad wouldn't get me a dog no matter what. It was a matter of principle. He got me a — well, it was sort of an electronic football game. You had to turn knobs to keep the other team from scoring."

"Is that how you broke your legs?" Carlie asked, looking at him sideways. "Turning those knobs?"

Harvey ignored her. "And then that Christmas I decided to get a guinea pig. I really still wanted a puppy but I knew better. And anyway a guinea pig was something else my mom had promised me. She raised guinea pigs when she was little. One time she had twenty-seven of them. She wanted to sell them to make money, but she couldn't bring herself to part with them."

"Whoo, that tells you something about people, doesn't it? They can't stand to part with stinking guinea pigs, but they throw their kids around like straws," Carlie said.

Harvey went on. "Anyway, I told my dad I wanted to buy my own Christmas present and he said, 'Fine with me.' And I went out and got a guinea pig — a big white one — I named him Snowball right there in the store."

"I know what's coming," Carlie said.

"And I got a cage, food, everything, and I brought him home, and my dad took one look at him, grabbed him up and carried him off. He said it was a matter of principle. He never would even tell me what he had done with Snowball."

"Some people."

"To make up for it he bought me a snooker pool table, but I never played with it."

"Matter of principle?" Carlie asked. She grinned at him. He didn't answer.

Thomas J cleared his throat. He said, "Every Christmas the twins gave me a present."

Both Carlie and Harvey turned and looked at Thomas J. Thomas J had never learned the art of talking because the Benson twins didn't say much. Sometimes their entire daily speech was "Water's boiling," and "Cronkite's on," and "I'm turning in." Therefore it was always a surprise to Carlie and Harvey when he joined in the conversation.

"What'd they give you?" Carlie asked.

"Well, one time it was pencils with my name on them."

"Oh, boo, that's the kind of thing you get for good behavior," Carlie said.

"How would you know?" Harvey asked.

Carlie grinned to herself. "Go on, Thomas J."

"Well, one time it was gloves and one time it was a book. *Big Bible Stories for Little People.*"

Thomas J fell silent. He remembered sitting beside one of the twins while she read the stories to him. He could see her gnarled finger holding the place on the page.

His favorite story had been about Baby Moses being sent out in a basket by his real mother to a better home. When he heard that story he always imagined his own mother waiting by the road, hiding in the poplar trees, waiting to see the twins take him in.

He wished he had thought to get the book while he was at the house with Mr. Mason. Suddenly he looked up. "Oh, yes, they also gave me three gold coins."

"Real gold?" Carlie asked.

He nodded.

"If I was you, I'd rub them against my skin. If your skin turns green, they aren't real. That's how I found out about my earrings. They turned my ears as green as that grass over there."

"Lunch," Mrs. Mason called.

"Whoo," Carlie said, getting up. "Don't tell me she managed to get lunch on the table without the slave of the world to help her. Things are looking up."

13

After lunch Harvey persuaded Carlie to push him to the library. "It's mostly uphill," Mrs. Mason said in a doubtful way.

"I don't care," Carlie said. "Harvey and me want to get some books, don't we, Harvey?" Carlie was willing to go anywhere and do anything. She was bored.

"It's very steep. The library's all the way at the top of Oak Street."

"I know where it is."

"And you won't take your hands off the chair for an instant?"

"Look, glue my fingers to the handles if it'll make you feel any better."

"I just want to be sure." She put her hand on the back of Carlie's neck. "And you'll be extra careful crossing the street?"

"I'm always careful with valuable things."

"Thank you," Harvey said.

She poked him. "I meant myself."

Mrs. Mason looked at them. "All right, but you be very careful, Carlie."

"Whoo, you'd think we were going to the North Pole."

They set out for the library with Carlie pushing Harvey in a slow rhythmic way. "I'd like to give Mrs. Mason a scare, wouldn't you?" Carlie asked. "We could get a dummy, dress him up in your clothes and push him down the street. I'd run after the wheelchair screaming 'Mrs. Mason, help, help. He got away from me!' I'd do it if it wasn't so hot."

"Mrs. Mason's all right," Harvey said.

"Well, she hasn't done us in yet." Carlie kept pushing. "That's what I'm going to do a list about — people who have done me in. If you did a list like that, how many people would be on your list? Don't give me every name, just guess at it."

Harvey thought of his mother and father. "Two," he said.

"I'd have, let's see — " Carlie pushed the chair slower as she thought. "First there would be my father. I mean, I don't know who he is, but he'd be first on the list.

"You don't have a father?" Harvey asked, looking back at her.

"Of course I have a father," she snapped. "Everybody has a father. The lowest dog in the street has a father. Didn't you learn anything in Health and Hygiene?" She stopped to ease his chair down the curbing. "I just never knew my father. He left before I was born. But my second father — "

"He would have to be your *step*father," Harvey corrected.

"He was a step *down* anyway," Carlie said. "He was a real bum. Number two on my list of people who have done me in would be that stepfather. Before he left he even stole my baby-sitting money."

Harvey was silent.

"Then my third father — *step*father, if you must — he was the first person who ever wanted to do me real harm. I mean, you're always hearing how dangerous the streets are and how you're going to get mugged or hit on the head? Well, in the streets I was perfectly safe. It was when I got home that I got mugged and attacked."

Harvey said in a quiet voice, "My father ran over my legs. That's how they got broken."

He spoke so quietly Carlie thought she hadn't heard right. "Ran over them?" She stopped pushing the wheelchair altogether.

"Yes."

"*Ran* over them?"

"Yes. In the car."

Her shoulders sagged. "Oh, wow."

"He said he couldn't help it."

"Which is supposed to make everything all right."

"He said he got mixed up on forward and reverse. He was drinking."

"Oh, wow."

"Yeah."

There was a silence. Then Carlie said, "You know, just think about this, Harvey. Just think about you and me as unborn babies. Here we are, see, waiting to be born. And somebody comes up to us with a pad and pencil and says 'What do you want in a father?'

"Well, we'd list all kinds of things. I'd say I want a father who's good-looking — after all, Harvey, half of your looks do come from your father — and I'd say I want a father who is rich and one who loves me. I'd go on and on." She rested herself against the back of Harvey's chair. "Never once would I think to say 'I want a father who will stick around.'

I mean, Harvey, he didn't even wait to see if I was a boy or a girl! He doesn't even know I'm *me*!"

She sighed. "And you, never once would you think to say 'I want a father who will know the difference between forward and reverse in a stupid car.'" She started pushing again, faster.

"I think that's the library up ahead," Harvey said.

"And then, Harvey, to make matters worse, here we are, totally unwanted — I think we have to admit that — and then there are people in the world who really want children and haven't got a one. Life is really unfair."

Harvey smiled a little. "That's something I have suspected for a long time."

14

"I thought you came to the library to check out books!" Carlie said. Ever since they had arrived, Harvey had been at a back table looking through old *New York Times Magazines*. Carlie had flipped through *Seventeen* and *Cosmopolitan*, and then she had gone to the librarian's desk.

"Do you have any movie magazines?"

"No."

"Comics?"

"No."

So now she was ready to go. "Get some books and let's leave," she said to Harvey impatiently.

"I'm staying until I find an article I'm looking for," Harvey said, turning the pages in a determined way.

"What's it about?"

"If you must know, the article is about my mother."

"What'd she do to get in the newspaper?"

"Well, she went to live on this farm in Virginia with some people. They were going to start a new way of life and that's what the article's about. I want to find out exactly where the farm is."

"What for?"

"So I can write her."

"Why don't you just ask your dad where the farm is. He's bound to know. He had to send the divorce papers somewhere."

"He wouldn't tell me. He won't even talk about her." He bent over the magazine again. "If my mom knew I was in a foster home — if she knew about these broken legs — well, she'd come get me. I know she would."

"And take you to the farm?"

"Yes."

"Where you'd live happily ever after?"

"Yes."

Carlie was silent for a moment. Then she said, "Didn't your mom ever write you?"

"Oh, sure, she wrote."

"Well, wasn't there any return address?"

"I never got the letters."

"Oh, sure, she wrote but you never got the letters. Just like my mom wrote but I never got the letters."

"No, she really wrote. I know she did, only my dad tore up the letters." He closed the magazine and picked up the next. "The article *has* to be in one of these."

"I'm getting bored," Carlie said. "Aren't there any cute boys in this town?" She spun around. "Hey, I think I'll go see if they have *Appalachian Nurse*." She went back to the desk.

Suddenly Harvey came upon the article about the farm. When he saw the picture of his mother making the hammock he felt as if his heart had blown up like a balloon.

His mother was looking down at the ropes. She had a serious look about her. There were four rings on her fingers, but no wedding ring.

He read the article carefully. Everyone at the farm, the article said, changed their names and selected other names that were more suitable to their nature. As near as he could figure out, his mother's new name was Bethenia.

In the evenings, he read, everyone at the farm sat around and had discussions. Some-times one person would sit in the center on a stool and offer himself for discussion. Every-one would then tell what they liked and didn't like about the person on the stool. Harvey had a hard time imagining his mother sitting there, letting herself be criticized. At home the least thing made her furious. If his father called her casserole "earth food," she sulked.

"Good news!" Carlie shouted coming toward him. "*Appalachian Nurse!*" She waved the book in his face. "And it starts out real good too. Listen to this: 'Nurse Laurie Myers made her way over the dark road. She was tired, but she knew men had been injured in the mine and needed her.'" Carlie glanced up. "Did you find what you were looking for?"

"Yes."

"Oh, let me see. Which one's your mother?"

"That one."

"I never pictured your mom looking like that. Hey, he's cute, the one on the left."

"She didn't look like that when she lived with us."

"Well, let's go then," she said impatiently.

"I want to get a Xerox copy first." He wheeled himself to the desk. "Can you copy this article for me?"

"It's ten cents a page."

"I've got the money right here." He dug into his pocket.

Carlie said, "Listen to this: 'In the depths of the mine lay Michael. One of his arms was caught under a mine timber.' " Carlie glanced up. "See, they're begging Laurie not to go in because of the danger, but she's going in anyway." She flipped through the pages. "This is really good. Here's the end. 'Michael looked at Laurie.' He must have got out of the mine all right. 'He took her in his arms.' See, Harvey, she even saved his arm! 'He said, "My life will always be yours because without you I would have no life."

" 'Laurie answered softly, "Without your love, there's no life for me either." They kissed.' " Carlie slammed the book shut. "Now, that's what I call a real satisfying story." She set it on the counter.

The librarian came back and said, "That will be ninety cents, please."

Harvey counted out the money and took the article about his mother. Carefully he got the pages in order.

As Carlie pushed him to the door he glanced up and said, "Oh, you forgot your book."

She looked at him, astonished. "I just read it. You saw me." She opened the door, held it with her shoulder and pushed him out into the sunlight. She sighed with satisfaction. "You know, it was almost as good as *Hong Kong Nurse*."

Harvey's father was coming for a visit, and Harvey was waiting on the front porch in his wheelchair. He was sitting as still as a statue.

"Carlie, let him see his father alone," Mrs. Mason said when she saw Carlie heading for the front porch.

"I will."

"Then stay in the house."

"I'm going for the *mail*," she said.

"The mail is already here. It's there on the desk."

"Anything for me?"

"No."

"For Harvey?"

"No."

"What's wrong with the mail these days anyway?" Carlie asked. "People are going to quit buying stamps if the post office doesn't start delivering letters." She kept going toward the porch.

"Carlie," Mrs. Mason warned. "I mean what I say. I don't want you out there when Harvey's father comes."

"I won't be. I'll come back in the house as soon as he gets here. I just want to get a look at the kind of creep who would run over his own son's legs."

"Who told you that, Carlie?"

"Harvey told me." She turned. "I wonder if he'll have the nerve to come driving up in the same car." Over her shoulder she said, "Anyway, when the creep comes, I will come right into the house. Girl Scout's honor."

Before Mrs. Mason could say anything else, Carlie went out onto the porch. She sat on the railing in front of Harvey.

Harvey was too nervous to fidget. He was sitting with his hands tightly clenched, his teeth clamped together. He had not seen his father since he came to the Masons', and the only thing he could remember about his father was him weeping in the emergency room. His tears, falling on Harvey's burning face, had seemed to sizzle.

"Is that his car?" Carlie asked.

"No."

"Because I'm supposed to go straight in the house as soon as he comes. Mason's orders." Carlie paused. She began swinging her feet back and forth. "Mail came. Nothing for you or me."

"I know."

"Hey, maybe your mom's not at the farm anymore. Did you ever think of that? She could be *anywhere*."

"Then I'll get my letter back. The return address was on it."

"I *know* my mom got my letters. She just won't answer. For all I know, she's left the state." Carlie kept swinging her legs back and forth, hitting the heels of her sandals against the railing. "If you weren't in that wheelchair, we could go looking for your mother."

"What?"

"Yeah," she said. She was pleased with the thought. "We could just take off. I'd really like to see the farm. I'm bored with this place anyway, aren't you?"

"Are you talking about running away again?"

Carlie looked at him. "Why do you have to make everything sound so bad? Run away. Nobody's going to *run away*. You been watching too many Shirley Temple movies. We're just going to take off, split." She glanced at the door to see if Mrs. Mason was within hearing, then she turned back to Harvey. "You know, it really isn't a bad idea, Harvey. I couldn't go home because they'd pick me right up, but this farm..."

"No."

"Why not?"

"For one thing, I am in a wheelchair in case you haven't noticed."

"Listen, the wheelchair would make it easier. It makes you look pitiful. Nobody would turn us down for a ride. I could step out and thumb and you could hold up a sign that said — "

"I couldn't do it."

"Harvey, you *could*. Listen — "

"I don't want to talk about it."

"But — "

"I don't want to talk about it!"

"All right, all right, we won't talk about it. You don't have to jump down my throat." She paused, then said, "Anything interesting in your lists lately?"

"What?"

"Your lists. Anything interesting?"

"Oh, no." Harvey's eyes were on the street. His father would have to come over the crest of the hill.

"What's your latest list about?"

"What? Oh." Harvey touched his forehead. He was too nervous to remember. He said, "Oh, I don't know. Let's see. Oh, yeah, it was just something I read that interested me, nothing important."

"What?"

"I read somewhere that one day everybody will be famous for fifteen minutes."

"Whoo, if that's true, I wish my fifteen minutes would hurry up and come. I am so bored."

"And I'm making a list of ways — if I get the fifteen minutes of fame — well, the ways I would want it to be."

"What do you want to do? Splash down in the Pacific in a rocket ship? Discover a new germ?" She straightened. "You know what I'd want? I'd want a fifteen-minute TV special. I'd come out in a low-cut, shiny dress like Cher and I'd be so good that everyone would say 'Who is she?' and 'She's going to be a star.'" Carlie grinned. "That way my fifteen minutes would just be the beginning of a whole lot of fifteen minutes. I'd stretch it out like an all-day sucker."

Harvey was still looking at the top of the hill. "I keep hearing a car but I don't see it."

Carlie said quickly, "How do *you* want to be famous?"

"I don't know. I forget what I put down now." He looked down at his legs. "I just hope it's not for something bad."

"Like what?"

"Oh, like maybe I've already had my fifteen minutes — maybe when my dad ran over my legs — " He looked at Carlie. "I mean, everybody in town knew about it. Everyone was talking. People were driving past our house. Maybe that was my fifteen minutes."

"Naw. They didn't just drive past your house for fifteen minutes, did they? Not if I know people. More like two or three days. No, you're going to be famous. Hey, you'll be a writer. I know you will. You'll write best-sellers."

"I don't know."

"Look, I was in the newspaper too one time, only they just called me a juvenile. You think I consider that fame? A juvenile? Naw, it's got to be more than that. You'll be a famous writer and then you can write a movie for me. I'll get to be a star that way."

"That's his car," Harvey said abruptly. He made a move as if he was trying to get to his feet. A pain shot through his legs.

"Are you sure?"

"It's the same car."

Carlie got to her feet. "Then I'll go inside as promised." At the door she turned. "If you need me, I'll be right inside the living room." She got serious. "You wouldn't believe, Harvey, what good help I can be in a fight."

16

Harvey watched his father coming up the walk. There was no expression on Harvey's face. Everyone had always told him that he looked exactly like his dad, and he realized it was true. Yet, inside, he had always felt more like his mother.

"Well, how's it going, Son?" his father asked. He took all three steps in one bound. Then he looked uneasy, as if he wished he'd taken more time.

"All right," Harvey said.

His father cleared his throat. "Looks like a nice place." His father was in the construction business — or had been until the building business went bad.

"It's all right."

"Any other kids here?"

"Two."

That sounds good — company." He paused

and cleared his throat again. Then he said more seriously, "What kind of kids are they?"

"They're all right."

"I mean, you know, kids in a foster home — well, you never know."

"*I'm* here," Harvey said.

"Oh, well, yeah." Harvey's father still had not looked directly at him. "And the legs?" he asked in a lower voice.

"They're all right," Harvey lied.

"Well, that's good news." He paused and then sat in the wicker rocker. He pulled at the turtleneck of his shirt. "Look, about the legs — " He still had not looked at Harvey.

"I don't want to talk about it."

"Well, I just don't know what got into me, that's all. Sure, I'd just lost a contract. Sure, I'd just had a couple of drinks. Sure, the car was new, but that still doesn't excuse it."

"No."

It was quiet on the porch now. Carlie had turned off the TV in the living room.

"Anyway, you seem to be getting on real well here," his father said with false cheer. "I've never seen you looking better."

"Except for the legs."

"Oh, well, yeah, sure." There was another silence. "Oh, guess what? I brought your birthday present — I didn't forget the big day's this Friday."

"Oh?"

"It's right out in the car only I'm not going to let you see me carry it in. You might guess what it is." His father got to his feet abruptly. "Well, what do you say? Let's go get something to eat."

"I don't know if I'm allowed."

"Sure you are — your own dad." He went to the door. "Mrs. Mason?"

Carlie's face popped into view as quick as a jumping jack's. "I'll get her." She ran into the dining room. "Mrs. Mason, Harvey's father wants to talk to you. He wants to know if he and Harvey can go get something to eat."

It was a relief to Harvey when his father left. He felt as flat as an old tire. He could hardly wheel himself into his room.

"How'd it go?" Carlie asked. She was leaning against the doorway in another halter. So far she had made eleven.

Harvey lifted his shoulders and let them drop.

"What does that mean?"

"It went all right," Harvey said in a flat voice. Actually it had never been all right, but the worst moment had come in the restaurant when Harvey had said, "I wrote a letter to my mother telling her what had happened." He hadn't planned to say it. It had just slipped out.

His father had swallowed hard and wiped his mouth with his paper napkin. "Did you?" he asked. There was no expression in his voice.

"Yes, but I haven't heard from her."

"You won't."

"I think I will." Harvey put down his fork and looked up at his father. He said, "She probably wrote to me dozens of times over the years only you never gave me the letters." This was something he had always suspected. He had even searched the trash cans for scraps.

"She never wrote you."

"I don't believe that." Harvey was holding his fork in both hands as if he was going to snap it in two. "She wrote and you tore up the letters. You probably flushed them down the toilet." He looked across the restaurant at a fat woman begging her thin son to eat just one more French fried potato.

"Look at me, son." Harvey's father's voice sounded so low and strange that he had to look. "She never wrote you," he said, "not one time." He pronounced every word carefully.

"She would write if she knew I had two broken legs."

"She didn't write when she knew you had the appendectomy."

"She didn't know about that."

"I wrote her."

"How about the measles?"

"I wrote her then too."

"And she didn't answer?"

"No."

"I don't believe you."

"*No!*"

As soon as his father said "No" in that way, Harvey knew it was true. He suddenly felt old and tired. He looked down at the fork in his hands. A moment before he had felt as if he could snap it in two. Now he could no longer even hold it. He let it drop to his plate.

He looked up at his father, taking in all his features. Maybe, he thought, it was because he looked so much like his father. Could his mother, hating his father, hate him too just because of his looks? She was always saying "You're your father's son," and he had known it was not a compliment — but could she hate him because of his looks?

"Eat your supper, Son."

"All right."

"Is your steak too tough?"

"No."

"Well, eat."

Harvey picked up his fork. He barely had the strength to move his baked potato. Finally he managed to cut his potato so it looked eaten, and to hide some of his steak, but he couldn't eat a bite.

Carlie was still standing in the doorway. "Where'd you eat?" she asked.

"Bonanza."

"Lucky! We had tuna casserole. One night I'm going to make tacos for everybody. Are they good!"

Carlie stood in the doorway, watching Harvey's back. Harvey was trying to get the strength to lift himself onto his bed. He wished for one of those special hospital lifting bars.

Carlie said, "Oh, by the way, one of the Benson twins died today — you know the old ladies Thomas J used to live with?" She came into the room. "Or did you hear about it?"

"No."

"Heart failure."

"Oh."

"It was Jefferson that died. Hey, and guess what the other twin's name was?"

"I can't."

"Thomas! Get it? Thomas and Jefferson! *Thomas Jefferson!*" She hooted with delight. "Whoo, how's that for names? You know, one time sombody told me they knew twins named Pen and Pencil, but I didn't believe it till now."

Harvey sat silent in his wheelchair, hunched forward like an old benched player.

"Thomas J is leaving in the morning to see the remaining twin and go to the funeral and all." She sighed. "Everybody here is having some excitement in their lives but me. You go off to Bonanza and Thomas J to a funeral."

She paused. Harvey was still staring at his bed. "I don't think I can make it," he said.

"What? Oh, you want to lie down? Here, I'll help you." She started forward.

"No, I don't think I can make it — period."

Carlie stopped in the middle of the room when she realized Harvey was talking about more than getting in bed. "Harvey, you *have* to make it."

"I really don't think I can."

"Because, Harvey, listen, you're one of us — you and me and Thomas J are a set. And

I've got used to you, Harvey. When I get used to somebody I don't want anything to happen to them."

She walked over to his wheelchair. "Look at me, Harvey — no, *look* at me."

He glanced up. His face was pale. His eyes were dull. His lips had a smudged look.

"I promise you can make it," she said.

He lowered his eyes.

"And I don't make promises easily, Harvey. Listen, I *promise* you can make it."

After a moment he said "I really don't think I can" in a flat quiet voice.

Carlie started at Harvey. Then she closed her eyes. She said, "You know, when I get my driver's license the first thing I'm going to do is find your father and run over *his* legs. See how *he* likes it."

She stamped out of the room and into the kitchen. "I never thought I'd say this, Mrs. Mason, but give me something to do."

"You want to work, Carlie?"

"I've got to take my anger out on something."

17

Thomas J didn't want to go back to the hospital. There was something upsetting about seeing only one twin, because the Benson twins had never been separated before in their lives. Other twins, Thomas J knew, went to different schools and wore different clothes, married different men and moved to different towns. But not the Bensons. They had stayed together and looked alike all their lives. They had never even worn different dresses. People took their picture in town sometimes.

As they drove to the hospital, Mr. Mason said, "I know this is hard for you, Thomas J. I remember my first funeral."

Thomas J looked up at him.

"It was an old man who worked for my father — Mr. Joe, they called him — and Mr. Joe was laid out in his house."

"I don't know what 'laid out' is."

"Well, it just means he was in his coffin there in his house."

"Oh."

"And I remember my daddy picked me up so I could see Mr. Joe in the coffin, and my knee must have hit the coffin and jarred it, and Mr. Joe's mouth came open. I never will forget that. I ran all the way home — seventeen blocks — hid under the bed."

"Oh."

"Kids don't do that anymore, hide under the bed, but we were always doing it if we were scared or wanted to cry without anybody seeing us."

Thomas J was quiet for a moment, and then he said, "It's not really the funeral that I'm worried about. I'm not scared about that."

"What are you worried about, Thomas J?"

"Well, going to the hospital."

"Why is that?"

"I don't know. It's something I can't put in words. It's just standing there and just one twin and all and not knowing what to say."

"Only sometimes you do a person a real

favor by standing there, Thomas J. Just the fact that you're there can be a comfort."

"I don't feel like a comfort," Thomas J said. He paused. "I want to say something but I can't. One of them's already dead and last time I didn't hardly say anything. I won't be able to say anything today either. I know I won't."

Mr. Mason looked at him. "I'll tell you something, Thomas J. I never told this to anybody in my life. But when I was your age my mother died. Now she was a good woman, real good, but she was never one to show affection."

"The twins were like that."

"I can never remember my mother hugging me or kissing me, not one time."

"I can't remember the twins doing that to me either. They patted me one time when I found their father's watch, on my head and shoulders, but . . ."

"The word 'love' was never mentioned in our house that I can remember."

"Mine either."

"So I went to the hospital and I was standing there by the bed, just like you, not able to say anything, and all of a sudden my mother opened her eyes and said 'Collin?' —

that's my first name. She said, 'Collin, tell me you love me.' Well, I just stood there like a stick. The word love had never been said to me in my whole life."

"Mine either."

"I mean, I know she loved me — I guess she did anyway — she took good care of me and I must have loved her, but I'd never said the word in my life."

"I haven't either."

"And so I just stood there. The nurse punched me in the back and said '*Say* it,' because she knew my mother was dying, and my dad yanked my arm and said '*Say* it!' I just stood there. I did love her, I guess, but my throat was as dry as sandpaper and I couldn't say a word."

"I couldn't have either."

"Well, finally the nurse — bless her heart — stepped up to the bed and said, 'He said it, Mrs. Mason! Did you hear him? He said it real soft but he said it. He loves you!' And my mother smiled and closed her eyes and that was the last time I ever saw her alive. To this day I am grateful to that nurse — Miss Brown, her name was — for helping me out."

"It *was* nice of her." Thomas J paused and thought. "I guess if mothers want you to tell them you love them, they should start real early, training you to do it." This was the longest and deepest speech Thomas J had ever made, and he looked quickly at Mr. Mason to see what he thought of it.

Mr. Mason was nodding. "I think you're right, Thomas J." He kept staring at the road ahead. "You know, I think that was one of the reasons I wanted to marry Ramona."

"Mrs. Mason?"

"Yes. Because she was always touching people and hugging them and telling them how she felt about them. It seemed to come so natural to her. It appealed to me."

"It should come natural."

"Would you believe it took five years of marriage — *five years* — before I could tell my own wife that I loved her?" Mr. Mason said.

"Yes," Thomas J replied earnestly. "I can believe it."

18

The remaining Benson twin lay with her eyes closed. Thomas J stood by her hospital bed waiting respectfully for her to open her eyes. It was a good feeling to have Mr. Mason behind him, now that he knew Mr. Mason had once, long ago, stood in front.

There was another woman in Jefferson's bed. She was flipping through a movie magazine, looking for a good article.

Finally Thomas J gave up and said, "Aunt Benson?"

One of her eyes snapped open. The other opened slowly.

"It's me, Thomas J."

"Thomas J?"

"Yes'm, the boy that lived with you for so long."

Her eyes focused on him. "Thomas J," she

said, "Sister's gone." Her voice, which had not been steady since 1945, wavered more than usual. She reached out her hand and he took it.

"I know."

Mr. Mason leaned over Thomas J's head. He put his hands on Thomas J's shoulders. "I brought him for the funeral, ma'am. He wanted to pay his respects."

"Sister and me had always planned a double funeral," she said. "We always said we was born together, we'd die together. When we broke our hips together, I was sure of it."

"Well," Mr. Mason said, "it just looks like you're going to have to stick around for a while — get the garden back in shape."

"Unless," she said, "I can manage to die before — " She broke off and made a feeble attempt to lift her head. "When's the funeral?"

"Two o'clock, but you — "

"Unless I can manage to die before two o'clock," she said, lying back on her pillow.

"It's twelve-fifteen now," the woman in the next bed said, folding her magazine to read an article about Liz Taylor's face-lift.

"Then I won't make it," the Benson twin said. She closed her eyes.

* * *

After the funeral, Mr. Mason remembered to pick up some Kentucky Fried Chicken. "It'll be a nice surprise," he said. "We forgot last time, remember? I thought they were going to tar and feather us."

Thomas J nodded. "Harvey'll be pleased." He moved closer to Mr. Mason on the car seat. He felt Mr. Mason's arm against his. He looked up at Mr. Mason. Suddenly Thomas J felt like somebody out of a book, a fairy tale, who had just stepped into real life and needed to know about it.

He said to Mr. Mason, "Tell me some more about the things that happened to you when you were little."

Carlie was washing the dishes hard. There were only a few of them so she was giving each her full attention.

Mrs. Mason smiled at her and said, "You don't have to wash off the flowers too."

"I can't help it," Carlie said. "Harvey's father makes me so mad. Harvey couldn't even eat his Kentucky Fried Chicken tonight."

The thought of sitting across the table from him and seeing him stare at his untasted drumstick made her wash the glasses even harder.

"Hey, if you don't want your chicken, I'll take it," Carlie had said to get a rise out of him. At her house a person would eat anything if he thought someone else wanted it.

But it hadn't worked with Harvey. Mutely he had handed her the drumstick.

She finished rinsing the glasses and dried her hands. "He just looks so sad sitting there staring out his window, and he's not pouting or sulking or anything, he's just sitting there."

"I know."

"You know, if they made a target of him — of the way he looks from the back and they set it up on the firing range — well, nobody could shoot it."

Mrs. Mason took the dishes from the drain and dried them in a slow careful way.

Carlie stared at the sink. "He looks like he's already been shot."

"Carlie," Mrs. Mason said, "do you remember me telling you that I thought you could help Harvey — this was about the second day you were here."

"I remember."

"Well, you have helped him."

Carlie glanced at Mrs. Mason in surprise. "How can anybody think he's been helped. He's worse!"

"He's worse now, at this moment, I know that, but you have helped him, Carlie."

Carlie shook her head. Her hair fell over her face as she turned away.

"It's odd about helping people. When I was your age the only person who could help me when I felt bad was my sister, Liz. She could always make me laugh. My other sister, Helen, is like me, more serious. Now, I'm not funny at all. I don't think I've ever said a comical thing in my life, and — "

"You're other things though."

"Thank you, Carlie." Mrs. Mason smiled. "Only what I mean is that you are helping Harvey, sometimes by just making him smile or feel better, and I don't want you to give up."

Carlie turned to Mrs. Mason. "I never give up on anybody I like," she said.

19

The next morning Harvey did not get out of bed. Carlie had come in several times to try and cheer him up, but nothing had worked.

Now she came in again. "Hey," she said, whispering in an excited way, "there's a big package for you in the hall closet."

"My birthday's this Friday," he said, staring at the upper bunk.

"This Friday? You didn't tell me that. Now, I'll have to get you something. What do you want? Name anything under fifteen cents and it's yours."

He didn't answer.

"Hey, I got an idea. Look, why don't you go ahead and open up your package now. Mrs.

Mason won't care, and it'll cheer you up."

"No."

"Well, then it might cheer me up. I'm beginning to feel lousy too. Want me to open it for you?"

"No."

"I don't mean open it all the way, I just mean *peek* at it. I can slip off the paper so carefully you wouldn't even know I had opened it. I do this all the time at Christmas."

"Go ahead if you want to."

"You mean it? You wouldn't mind?"

"No."

"Whoo, I love opening presents. I don't even care whether they're mine or not." She went to the hall closet and slid out the box. "It's a big one," she called to Harvey. "The bigger the better, I always say." She pulled off the ribbon, which was punched into the top of the box. With great care she undid the strips of Scotch tape. She opened the end. When she saw that it was a portable color television set, her breath eased out in one long sigh.

"Oh, wow," she called to Harvey, "you're going to really like this."

Carefully she retaped the paper, punched the bow back in the original hole and slid the box back into the closet. Then she went back to Harvey's room and leaned against the bed. "Guess what it is?" she said.

"A TV."

"What?"

"A TV."

She was startled. She tried to bluff. "What makes you think it's a TV?"

"I saw my father carrying it in."

"Well, I'm not saying whether it is or it isn't," she said. She was disappointed. She loved to make people guess things. She had been looking forward to a long session with Harvey.

He would say, "Is it something useful?"

She would say, "Yes."

"Is it different colors?"

"*Definitely* yes."

"Does it move?"

"Well, *it* doesn't, but something *about* it does."

Now the game was ruined. She glanced down and Harvey looked so miserable that she forgave him. She knelt by the bed. "You know, if you really want me to, I'll go to that farm in Virginia, Harvey, and get your mother."

"No."

"But I wouldn't mind. Really. I could make

a hammock or two while I'm there. Bring you one for your birthday."

"No."

She got serious. "Look, Harvey, if your mother knew that you had these broken legs and that your father did it, she'd come get you. I know she would, and I — "

"*No!*"

"Well, I can go if I want to, Harvey, you can't stop me."

"*No!*"

The word was so agonized that Carlie stepped back from the bed. She stayed without speaking for a moment, then she stepped forward. "Oh, look," she said. "I got some little decals and put them on my fingernails. Did you notice?" She waved her fingers in front of Harvey's face. He closed his eyes.

"I saw them."

"Want me to put some on your toenails?"

"No."

"Just on your big toenails then. Oh, come on. It'll be fun." She yanked down the sheet. "People always look at your legs because they stick out and the decals would be a nice touch. Give them a smile. What would you rather have — flowers or little black poodles?"

"No."

Carlie bent closer. She looked at his feet.

"Hey, wait a minute, she said. "Did you know that your right toes are redder than your left ones? And they're all swollen." –

"I don't care."

"They look terrible. Doesn't your leg hurt?"

"No."

"It does too. I'm getting Mrs. Mason."

"I'm fine!"

Carlie ran from the room. "Mrs. Mason, come look at Harvey's toes. I'm no nurse yet, but I know bad-looking toes when I see them, and these are bad-looking toes."

20

Carlie and Thomas J were sitting on the front
steps, waiting for Mrs. Mason and Harvey to
get back from the hospital.

"I knew there was something wrong as soon
as I saw those toes," Carlie was saying.

"I didn't see them, but I knew something
was wrong."

"I hope they just have to give him a shot
or some pills. His birthday's Friday."

"I don't know when my birthday is,"
Thomas J said.

"Well, mine's August seventh, and don't
forget it. That's just three and a half weeks
away."

"I won't forget."

"Even if I'm gone, you send me something."

"I'll be glad to."

"And I'll make you up a birthday. You can have the same day as me if you want — August seventh."

"All right." The thought of his own birthday made him smile to himself.

"And how old you want to be? Eight? Nine?"

"Nine sounds good."

"Nine it is." She looked up the street. "I wonder what's keeping them. It's been two hours. Even *I* could give a shot in less than two hours and I haven't even had nurse's training yet."

"Maybe he'll have to stay in the hospital like the Benson twins." Thomas J's good feeling about having a birthday and being nine left him.

"Well, if he does, I sure hope they take better care of him. One of them died."

"I know."

"When I get to be a nurse, none of my patients are going to die. I'm going to make it real clear — *no dying!* I'll get to be like — oh, like a good-luck nurse. People will ask for me — especially real sick people — because they'll know my Number One Rule. No dy-

ing!" She got to her feet. "Here they come —
oh, it's only Mrs. Mason." She ran to the
driveway. "Where's Harvey?"

"They're keeping him in the hospital. The
leg's infected."

"Is it bad?"

"It's pretty bad, Carlie. And the worst
thing is that he just doesn't seem to care."

"It's that father of his. When I get my
driver's license I'm going looking for him.

"Now, Carlie."

"Well, Harvey's been like that ever since
his father came for that stinking visit."

"The man's got problems, Carlie."

"Sure the man's got problems. Everybody's
got problems, only they don't run over their
kid's legs because of them." She turned to
Thomas J. "We'll go see him right after supper and cheer him up."

"I'm not very good at that sort of thing,"
Thomas J said, recalling his failure with the
Bensons.

"Well, you better get good at it pretty quick.
I am not going to have Harvey lying up there
in misery with his birthday this Friday. I
was planning to bake him a cake."

"You can still bake the cake and take it to
the hospital," Mrs. Mason said.

"It won't be the same. A birthday away from home is bad enough, but a birthday in the hospital! Whoo! My birthday's coming up in three and a half weeks and I better be home for it. I better get a floating opal too." She started for the kitchen. "And Thomas J's birthday is the same as mine, isn't it, Thomas J?"

"Yes."

"And he's going to be nine, aren't you, Thomas J?"

"Yes, nine," he said firmly. He followed her into the kitchen.

21

Harvey was in a room by himself. He was, as
Carlie had known he would be, staring up at
the ceiling. When Carlie and Thomas J entered, they bumped into each other. They had
known he would look bad, but not that bad.

"Well, look who's come to visit you!" Carlie
said.

Harvey turned his head to them. There was
no expression on his face, but his lips were
in a straighter line than usual.

"How're you feeling?" Carlie asked, coming closer.

"All right."

"Want me to roll up your bed?" she asked.
"I love to do that. When I get to be a nurse

I'm going to spend all my time rolling people up and down."

"No thanks."

"Oh, well, want a drink of water then? Look, Thomas J, they have special straws that bend."

"The Benson twins had those."

Carlie shot him a hard look. "Want a drink, Harvey?"

"No."

"Well, can I have one then? I haven't got anything catching."

As she bent to drink, she suddenly straightened. "Hey, I'm going to have a surprise for you on your birthday. I'm not telling what it is, but I'm making it myself." She paused, waited, then asked, "Want to guess?"

"No."

"Okay, I'll give you a hint. This thing I'm giving you is very useful and it's also a thing of great beauty. Go ahead. Try and guess."

Harvey was silent.

"Ask me questions. Come on. Ask things like 'What color is it?' "

"What color is it?"

"Ah, the guessing is underway. The colors are black and white and pink and yellow." She nudged Thomas J and grinned. Thomas J looked so puzzled that she leaned down and whispered, "It's a *chocolate* cake with *white* icing, *pink* candles and *yellow* flames. Now don't give it away." She stood at the foot of the bed, waiting. Harvey was looking at the ceiling.

"I don't think he's going to guess," Thomas J said.

Carlie said, "Well, if you really don't want to guess, we'll just wait and let it be a surprise." She moved around the bed. "Oh, guess what happened today? This was so stupid. The phone rang and I picked it up and said, 'Hello,' and this girl's voice said, 'Hi, how are you?' I said, 'Oh, I'm fine, how are you?' And she said, 'Fine, what you doing?' I said, 'Nothing much, how about you?' She said, 'Watching TV, only nothing good's on.' I said, 'It never is.' Then there was a real long pause and she said in a kind of funny voice, 'You know, I think maybe I've got the wrong number. Is this Marcie?' I said, 'No, it's Carlie.' And we hung up. I should have known nobody in this town would call me. Wasn't that the stupidest thing. I almost died!"

Harvey didn't answer.

Thomas J cleared his throat and said, "Mr. Mason's going to take me fishing."

"And you too, Harvey, soon as your legs get well," Carlie said. "Although if it was me and I knew I'd have to go fishing when I got cured, I'd probably just stay on in the hospital." There was a pause and then Carlie said, "Hey, did I show you my decals?" She held out her hands, then let them drop. "Oh, yeah, I did. Anyway I'm glad you got to see them this afternoon because when I was making peanut-butter-and-mayonnaise sandwiches for me and Thomas J, I dropped some mayonnaise on my nails and the decals melted." She held out her hands. "It's probably something in the mayonnaise."

There was another silence. Carlie was still trying to think of something to say when the nurse put her head in the door. "Visiting hours are over."

"But we just got here," Carlie protested.

"You can come back tomorrow."

"Just give me five more minutes," Carlie begged. She could not bear to leave without cheering Harvey up. She looked at him. His face was still turned to the ceiling. She wanted to say something funny. She wanted to make Harvey laugh out loud. "Thomas J," she said through her teeth. He shrugged helplessly.

Carlie knew she was on her own. She tried

to think of something funny that had happened to someone else. Then she could turn it around and say it had happened to her. She did that all the time. But now her mind was blank.

"Well, we better go," she said. She leaned over the bed. "Listen, everything will be all right," she said. "I promise it will." Then she turned to Thomas J and said, "Come on, the nurse'll be chasing us out of here with hypodermic needles in a minute."

They walked down the hall and out the front door of the hospital. "Well, Thomas J, you and me are failures at being cheerer-uppers."

"I always have been," he said.

"Well, I haven't. I expected better of myself." Carlie pulled her shoulders back. "Listen, all night you think of funny things to say and talk about, and I'll do the same. Tomorrow we'll be funny enough to go on 'Hollywood Squares.'"

"I won't."

She turned and grabbed him by the shoulders. "Listen, tomorrow we are going to say funny things and I mean it. Right?"

"Right," Thomas J answered.

22

It was Thursday night and Harvey was worse. Now he wouldn't even speak to anyone. The nurses had started feeding him through a tube in his arm.

Harvey's father had come on Wednesday and sat with him for over an hour. He had told the doctors in a loud voice that money was no object. He told them they could spend whatever they had to and he would foot the bill. He said he had just gotten a contract to build an eight-unit town house.

"We're doing all we can now," one of the doctors had answered.

Carlie was furious when she heard about it. "You mean they let that rotten bum come in Harvey's room?"

"It's his father, Carlie."

"Whoo, next thing you know they'll be letting germs and viruses in."

That night when everyone was in bed at the Mason house, Carlie got up. She slipped into Thomas J's room and shone a flashlight in his face. "You asleep?"

He put his hand up to block out the light. "No, I was just lying here thinking."

"About Harvey?"

"Yeah. I'm used to him being on the bottom bunk and shifting around and all. I can't get to sleep without him. It's too quiet."

"Me either. Now, listen, I got an idea. You want to go in cahoots with me?"

Thomas J wasn't sure what that was, but he said, "I'd be glad to."

"All right, look, I went through the newspaper after supper and guess what I found in the ads!"

"What?"

"Look, it's right here." She shone the light on the folded newspaper. "Can you read it?"

Thomas J bent closer to the paper. Carlie was too impatient to wait for his eyes to focus. She read it herself. "Puppies free to good homes!"

"Puppies?"

"Yeah, Thomas J, we're going to go right over there first thing in the morning and get Harvey a puppy."

Thomas J couldn't seem to take it in. "A *puppy*?"

"Yeah, he's always wanted one — remember? It was the first thing on his list. And it'll cure him, Thomas J, I know it will. Why, if I was in the hospital half-dead and somebody hooked a floating opal around my neck, I'd get up and do the hula." She broke off. "And the best part is they're free. See? *Free* to good homes."

"But is this a good home?"

"If it's good enough for us, it's good enough for a dog, isn't it?"

"What about Mrs. Mason though? She might get mad."

"I'll take all the responsibility. I'm used to people being mad at me. It doesn't bother me a bit. I'll say I forced you to come with me and — "

"No, I want to come on my own. She can get mad at me too."

"All right then, after breakfast we'll go over to Woodland Circle — wherever that is — and we'll take a shopping bag — see, we'll have to sneak him into the hospital — and we'll pick out a puppy and take him over to the hospital and pull him out and sing 'Happy Birthday to You.' How does that sound?"

"It sounds good to me."

"I know it'll cure him. I mean, who is going to lie there staring up at the ceiling when a puppy is licking his face? It just can't be done."

"What if the puppy doesn't lick him though?"

"We'll pick one that will. After all, there're bound to be — how many puppies in a litter — six? Seven? There's bound to be one licker." At the door she paused and said, "Not a word of this to Mrs. Mason, you hear me?"

"Yes."

"Or Mr. Mason." Carlie sensed the bond that had grown between them.

There was a pause, then, "All right."

"See you in the morning."

23

Carlie and Thomas J walked slowly down the hospital hall with the shopping bag between them. "I wish he wasn't such a wiggler," Carlie said, looking straight ahead.

"That's why you picked him — because he was the liveliest one."

"I know, but I feel like we got a tiger in there, the way the bag's shaking. I'm afraid he's going to bust out the bottom."

"If he wets, I know he will."

"Don't even think such things," Carlie said. "And remember, every time you see a nurse, get in front of the bag. Nurses are known for their sharp eyes. Doctors aren't. We could bring an elephant in here and the doctors wouldn't notice."

Thomas J and Carlie went straight to Harvey's room. "Shut the door, shut the door," Carlie said quickly.

She ran over to Harvey's bed. He was staring at the ceiling. "Hey, it's just me, Carlie. You can look at me in safety. I'm not wearing one of my famous halters." He turned his eyes to her. "See, I lied." She grinned. "I've got on my shocking-pink one — your favorite." Before he could look back at the ceiling she said, "Hey, we brought you something."

Harvey didn't speak.

"And I'm not even going to make you guess what it is. I'm just going to tell you that it is fat, spotted, wiggly, that it has a tail and a pink nose and that it is dying to get out of this shopping bag." She reached down and brought up the puppy. "Taa-dah! Puppy-time!"

Carlie nudged Thomas J. "Happy Birthday to you, Happy Birthday to you, Happy Birthday, dear Haaaaaarvey, Happy Birthday to you."

There was a silence. Thomas J said, "We wanted to get a white one so we could name him Snowball, but they all had spots on them."

Carlie set the puppy on the bed beside Harvey. She nudged him forward.

Delighted to be out of the bag, the puppy rushed for the nearest face — Harvey's — and began licking his neck.

Carlie looked at Thomas J and rolled her eyes upward. "Thank goodness," she mouthed.

Harvey didn't move. "Don't you like him, Harvey?" Thomas J asked. It was the first present he had ever been in on. He wanted more than anything that it be a success. "He's real nice — and fat too," Thomas J said. "Feel him."

"Yeah, pleasingly plump is not the word," Carlie said.

"And soft too," Thomas J said anxiously.

Harvey did not move. Thomas J squinted up at Carlie. "Should we sing the birthday song again?"

Suddenly Harvey lifted his hand. He laid it on the puppy.

"I don't think so." Carlie grinned.

Harvey spoke for the first time in two days. "Is this for me?" he asked.

"Compliments of Carlie and Thomas J," Carlie said.

"It's mine?"

"Yeah, it's your birthday present. We picked it out special."

"Permanently?"

"Sure, what kind of gifts do you think me and Thomas J give? If we'd wanted to give you something unpermanent we'd have gotten a Popsicle."

"I can keep him?"

"Yeah, sure, what else? As a matter of fact, he's unreturnable."

The puppy was wiggling against Harvey's neck, and suddenly Harvey started to cry. It was the first time he had cried since the accident. It was like the turning on of a spigot. He sobbed, and the tears rolled down his cheeks in streams. The puppy, wild with all the excitement, licked at the tears.

"Go ahead and cry all you want to," Carlie said happily. "You got your own personal crying towel now." She turned to Thomas J. "You know, when I get to be a nurse, every morning I'm going to bring a basket of puppies to the hospital with me. They're better than pills."

Harvey was still crying. "It just makes me feel so — " He broke off. "I don't know. It's just that I didn't think — oh, I don't know how I feel." He cried again.

The nurse on the floor was passing the door and heard the commotion. She stuck her head in the room.

"Under the covers, quick!" Carlie said, poking the puppy under the sheet.

"What's going on in there?"

"Believe it or not," Carlie said, "we are having a wonderful time."

The nurse kept looking at Harvey. She said, "Harvey, are you all right?"

"Yes'm."

"Are you laughing or crying?"

"Both, I guess."

The nurse kept standing there. She noticed the bulge under the sheet, but she decided to ignore it. This was the first time Harvey had shown any sign of life in two days. "You want anything?" she asked.

"No."

"Cokes," Carlie hissed at him.

"Oh, yeah, could me and my friends have a Coke?" Harvey asked. "It's my birthday." He wiped his remaining tears on the sheet.

"Of course."

"Want to see what I got for my birthday? My friends gave it to me."

"Don't — " Carlie started to say, but Harvey reached under the sheet and pulled out the puppy before she could finish.

"Now, you know better than to have a puppy in here," the nurse said. "Why, if I had seen that puppy I would have to send him out right this minute."

"Yes'm."

She smiled. "I'll bring the Cokes." She started out the door and then leaned back in. "And many happy returns of the day, Harvey."

"Thank you." As the door closed, he held up the puppy so he could get a good look now that his eyes were dry. "This is the nicest puppy I have ever seen."

"Thomas J and me only give the best," Carlie said.

"There was six of them," Thomas J said, "but this one came running over and started licking us and we knew it was the one for you."

Carlie said, "Listen, don't think this puppy is *all* you're getting for your birthday though. I'm making my famous mayonnaise cake and bringing it over tonight."

"And will you bring the puppy back then too?"

"Listen, this puppy is not so easy to lug around," Carlie said. "If you want to do any real playing with him, you're going to have to get out of this hospital."

"I will," Harvey said, "but will you bring him tonight?"

"*If*," Carlie said, "Mrs. Mason will lend me her tote bag."

24

"Well, that's what's known as a successful gift, Thomas J," Carlie said. They were walking home from the hospital with the puppy between them.

"Yeah."

Carlie threw back her head and breathed in the morning air. "You know, Thomas J, I just feel real good."

"Me too."

"This is probably what it feels like to be famous."

"Famous?"

"Yeah — hey, get the puppy, will you, he's going under those bushes." She waited, then said, "Like one time Harvey was making up one of his lists and he was deciding how he wanted to be famous — he said that one day everybody will be famous for fifteen minutes — and he was figuring out what he wanted his fifteen minutes to be like."

"What did he decide?" Thomas J paused to pull the puppy back on the sidewalk. "This is really a nice little puppy."

"Oh, I can't remember. I think he wanted to be an astronaut and land on the moon, something like that. Or write a best-seller. Anyway, the point is, Thomas J, that this is probably what we'll feel like when we get famous."

"Yeah."

"A preview of coming attractions. Nice feeling, isn't it?"

"I think this puppy's getting to know me. Look how he follows."

"Anyway," Carlie went on, "until I do get famous, Thomas J, fifteen minutes like this every now and then will keep me going."

They could see the Masons' house in the distance, and they both got silent. Finally Thomas J said, "How are we going to tell Mrs. Mason what we did?"

"How do you think we're going to do it?" she snapped. "Write it in the air with a sparkler?" She straightened. "We're going to walk in and say 'Look what we got Harvey for his birthday.' Anyway, don't worry about it. Anybody that would take *us* in, isn't going to turn away a puppy."

"I hope not."

"Plus the fact that Mrs. Mason has been real worried about Harvey. I heard her talking to Mr. Mason — it was like he was their real child they were so worried."

Carlie opened the screen door and went into the house. She could hear the mixer going in the kitchen, so she went in and said, "Hey, look what we got Harvey for his birthday!" She held up the puppy. She didn't sound as confident as she had when she had been outside on the sidewalk.

Mrs. Mason looked at the puppy. She wiped her hands on her apron. She said, "Now who thought of that?"

"I did," Carile said. She stepped a little in front of Thomas J.

"But I helped," Thomas J said, accepting his part of the blame.

"Why, what a lovely thing to do!" Mrs. Mason came over and hugged Thomas J and Carlie, one in each arm.

In the curve of her arm, Thomas J felt like a stick. He wanted to say "What a lovely thing for *you* to do too," but he couldn't.

He remembered a talk he and Mr. Mason had had. You can't just blurt out things about love, they had decided, without some training.

Thomas J wished suddenly he had had some training. He thought of himself on an imaginary mother's lap.

"Who do you love?" she would say.

He would not know the answer.

"Well, do you love Ma-ma?" she would prompt.

"Yes."

"Then say it."

"I love Ma-ma."

"Say it again, real loud."

"I love Ma-ma."

Later, maybe, Thomas J thought, with a little training from Mrs. Mason he could learn to say something nice, even if it wasn't the word "love."

Mrs. Mason stepped back. "We'll have to tell Harvey about the puppy. It'll give him something to look forward to. We can take a picture of him with the Polaroid and — "

"He already knows."

"You didn't take it to the hospital?"

"Yes."

"Why, the nurses would have had a fit if they'd seen it."

"No, there was one real nice nurse — I'm going to copy myself after her — and she saw it but pretended not to," Carlie said.

"And did it perk him up?" Mrs. Mason asked.

"Oh, yeah, he cried at first," Carlie said, "but it wasn't a bad sort of crying, and then he sat up — I rolled up the bed in my best professional manner — and we all had Cokes. It was a real happy occasion."

"Harvey needs a few of those."

"Later I'm going to make my famous mayonnaise cake — it's the best thing you ever ate — you can't even taste the mayonnaise — and take it over. I'm going to put candles on it and silver Decorettes — the works."

"Listen, I've got an idea," Mrs. Mason said. "Why don't you two go down to the grocery store — they have pet supplies there — and get, oh, a little collar and a leash, maybe a toy bone or something, and we'll wrap them up as gifts and take them over with the cake."

"And worm pills!" Carlie said. "That'll be funny. Come on, Thomas J." At the door she paused. "This is going to be a really nice birthday." She grinned. "Just remember me and Thomas J have one coming up in three weeks, haven't we, Thomas J?"

"Yes," Thomas J said, "August seventh."

Then she and Thomas J went out the door.

25

The remaining Benson twin, Thomas, died on Monday, and it was decided that Thomas J should have a haircut before going to the funeral. In the barbershop he felt his first sadness about her death.

He had climbed up into the chair, excited at his first real haircut, and the barber had looked at him and said, "Who's been hacking at your hair, Son?" in an uncomplimentary way.

As soon as the barber said that, Thomas J had been once again on the Benson farm with the twins clipping away at his head as if it were a bush. He had closed his eyes, lost in unhappiness.

"There!" the twins would cry. They always finished at the same time. He never knew what he would look like till he got to the bathroom mirror.

The barber had brushed him off and said, "Now, you're a real nice-looking young man, if I do say so myself."

Thomas J had opened his eyes. Looking at the neatly trimmed boy in the mirror — the two halves the same at last — he had felt his sorrow draining from him.

Now, seated beside Mr. Mason in the car, he felt only pleasure in an outing with Mr. Mason.

"Mr. Mason?"

"What?"

Thomas J paused.

"What is it, Thomas J?"

Thomas J wanted to bring up some problem so that Mr. Mason would say "I know how you feel, Thomas J, because the same thing happened to me. Let me tell you about it." Only Thomas J couldn't think of a problem.

"Oh, nothing," he said. He looked out the window. He saw the reflection of his own face, neatly framed in the new haircut.

"Did I ever tell you about the time my daddy took me to Bear Rocks and I got lost?"

Thomas J turned to him, his face bright. "No."

"Well, one time — I was just about your age — and my daddy got the idea that we should . . ."

Thomas J and Mr. Mason stood looking at the Benson twin in her coffin. She was wearing her good black dress and her cameo pin, the same outfit her sister had worn. Thomas J was glad about that.

Mr. Mason put one hand on Thomas J's shoulder. "You know, Thomas J, they thought they were doing you a kindness when they took you in. You should always remember that."

Thomas J looked up at Mr. Mason. "They *were* doing me a kindness."

Mr. Mason nodded. "I'm sure they thought so."

Thomas J looked back at the Benson twin. Now, dead at age eighty-eight, she actually resembled the president for whom she had been named. "I'll remember," Thomas J said.

"Well, Thomas J is off to another funeral," Carlie said as she settled on the foot of Harvey's hospital bed. "It's a good thing they weren't triplets."

130

Harvey was lying with the head of his bed rolled up. "How's my dog?" Every time he mentioned his dog, he felt good. He had even told his father when he came for a visit. "I have a dog now," he'd said, looking right into his father's eyes. All his father had said was "That's all right."

"Oh, your dog's fine," Carlie said. "He went on the paper two times yesterday. You know, Harvey, you're beginning to look like yourself again."

"Too bad I can't look like somebody else, huh?"

"No, I like the way you look. Hey, wait a minute, I've got an idea. Comb your hair down in bangs."

"No."

"But I think you'd look good in bangs, and then push your glasses up on top of your head, Hollywood style."

"I can't see without my glasses."

"Well, I'll tell you how you look. Come on." There was a pause while Harvey brushed his hair over his forehead. "Now put your glasses on your head." Carlie looked at him with her head to one side. "Harvey," she said.

"What?"

"Put your glasses back on your face and your hair back on your head."

With a faint smile he brushed back his hair and put on his glasses.

"And one other thing, Harvey."

"What?"

"Promise me you won't ever try to look like anybody but yourself again."

Harvey smiled. "I promise."

26

Carlie and Thomas J were sitting on the steps of the elementary school building. The puppy was lying at their feet, resting from the walk. A fly landed on him and he twitched his ear to shake it off. The fly walked onto his forehead. The puppy raised his head and snapped at the fly. He watched as it flew away. Then he went back to sleep.

Carlie looked at Thomas J. "Thomas J, this is where you'll go to school at the end of the month," she said.

"In this building?" He looked around.

"Yeah, Harvey and me will go over on Oak Street. Harvey swears he can help me pass math, but I don't know."

"I'll be glad to go to this school."

"I'd like to go to nurse's school. The last school I went to was mostly made up of snobs. If you didn't have a certain kind of shoes or a certain kind of clothes — which I never had — nobody would speak to you."

They sat in silence for a moment. Thomas J was still looking back in admiration at his school. Carlie reached out and rocked the puppy with her bare feet.

"You know, Thomas J," she said, "wouldn't it be nice if we could get to our brains with an eraser?"

"What?" He looked at her, puzzled. "Did you say eraser?"

"Yeah. I just mean that there are things I don't like to remember — oh, like times people snubbed me at school — times people made me feel bad — and if I could just erase those things, Thomas J, I'd be a lot happier. Wouldn't you like to have a brain as perfect as a melon — no bad spots at all?"

"I don't have enough to remember," Thomas J said.

Carlie looked at him. "Can't you remember your mother at all?"

"No — well, sometimes when I see a woman who is kind of fat — no, not fat, just kind of . . ."

"Plump?"

"No, just the kind of woman who looks like, well, if you climbed up in her lap, well, you would be very comfortable."

"Oh."

"So every time I see a woman like that and she has on a flowered dress, well, it makes me want to go over and stand beside her."

"You probably had a mother who had a comfortable lap and wore flowered dresses."

"Yes." It was a sigh.

Carlie was still looking at him. "I could make you up a mother, Thomas J," she said, "like I made you up a birthday."

Thomas J hesitated. He was tempted. In his mind the picture of the woman in the flowered dress sharpened. He could almost see her. Then abruptly he shook his head.

"But I wouldn't mind," Carlie went on.

"I know, but I have a real mother," he said, "somewhere."

"Me too, somewhere," Carlie said. "Only she couldn't care less."

Thomas J looked at her in surprise. He said, "I can imagine somebody not wanting me, but I can't imagine anybody not wanting you."

She looked at him. "Thomas J, that was a real nice thing for you to say."

"Thank you." A small smile came over his face.

"Anyway, Thomas J, when you get older you can find your mother. Being pinballs is just a stage we're going through and — "

He squinted at her. "I don't know what pinballs are."

"You never played a pinball machine? Well, I'll take you to this place in town I know and we'll play." She looked up abruptly. "No, I take that back, Thomas J."

"About me finding my mother?" he asked, startled.

"No, I really think you can do that."

"About us playing pinballs?"

"No, about us *being* pinballs. That's what I was wrong about. You'll see what I'm talking about when you play the game. We are not pinballs." She grinned. "Don't ever let anybody call you a pinball, Thomas J."

"I don't know what you're talking about."

"Oh, nothing. It's just that pinballs can't help what happens to them and you and me can. See, when I first came here, all I thought about was running away, only I never did it." She looked at Thomas J. "I know that doesn't sound like much, but it was me deciding something about my life. And now I have decided that when I go to this new school, I'm really going to try. And you, you're really going to try too, aren't you?"

He nodded.

"And as long as we are trying, Thomas J, we are not pinballs."

They looked at each other. The fly had started bothering the puppy again, and he snapped at it. He got to his feet and looked around for something to chew. He tumbled over Carlie's feet and grabbed Thomas J's sock. He began to tug.

Carlie stood up. "It's time to go."

"Yes," Thomas J said. He unhooked the puppy's teeth from his sock and got to his feet. "Let's go home."

About the Author

Betsy Byars began writing as her own four children
were growing up and her many titles have won her
wide recognition and an enthusiastic audience. She
is the author of *The Summer of the Swans*, which
received the Newbery Award.

The Pinballs was an ABC After School Special. Two
other books by Betsy Byars, *Goodbye, Chicken Little*
and *Trouble River* are also available in APPLE
PAPERBACK editions.

Ms. Byars grew up in North Carolina and now lives
in South Carolina. She and her husband have traveled
widely throughout the United States pursuing their
interest in gliding and antique airplanes.